Something is not quite right. . .and it just got worse.

"That Turner definitely reminds me of someone," Steve said. "The more I see of him, the more it strikes me. But for the life of me I can't put a name to him."

Suddenly, a shot shattered the afternoon stillness. The four horses pulling the buckboard instantly bolted. They charged down the rough trail as though driven by an insane wagon master. Bracing her feet against the front of the wagon, Megan gripped the seat, her knuckles white, trying to stay aboard.

"Whoa!" Steve shouted frantically. "Whoa!" Raising the reins high, he leaned back on the lines with all his might, but still the horses ran. The rushing wind caught Steve's hat, sending it sailing. The plain was a brown blur. On and on the buckboard flew, bouncing, swaying, careening down the trail.

Frothing at the mouth, eyes wild, the horses bounded on. Megan's arms ached from clinging to the seat. She knew she couldn't hold on much longer.

The front wheel on her side slid into a small gully, and she felt the wagon tilt. Scrambling, clawing for a hold, she heard the splinter of cracking wood and the terrified scream of a horse. The buckboard fell heavily on its side, throwing her to the stony ground. She had the sensation of falling, felt a stabbing pain in her right shoulder, and everything went black.

ROSEY DOW makes her **Heartsong Presents** debut with *Megan's Choice*, her first inspirational romance novel. Although Rosey writes about the Colorado territory as if she is right there, she resides with her family as missionaries in Grenada, West Indies.

Megan's Choice

Rosey Dow

Heartsong Presents

To Dave,
my husband and best friend.

A note from the Author:
I love to hear from my readers! You may write to me at
the following address: **Rosey Dow**
Author Relations
P.O. Box 719
Uhrichsville, OH 44683

ISBN 1-55748-972-6

MEGAN'S CHOICE

Cover illustration by Victoria Lisi and Julius.

PRINTED IN THE U.S.A.

one

"Mr. Steven Chamberlin, please," Megan Wescott told the lanky hotel clerk. She had a pleasant, poised voice. It didn't give away the secret that her stomach was full of flying butterflies.

The young clerk gave her a friendly smile as his eyes approved of her large, brown eyes and creamy complexion. "One moment, please," he replied and held up his hand to summon a bellboy. "You can wait inside if you like."

Glancing around, Megan entered the hotel lobby to wait. The grandeur of the hotel snatched away her breath for an instant. She hesitated inside the door, feeling out of place and alone. She wished she could slip her hand into the warm shelter of her father's coat pocket, her habit as a child whenever she was troubled or frightened. If only he were here to help her now.

But she was no longer a child. Daddy was gone, and she would have to look after herself. And Jeremy.

"A-hem."

She realized a woman in a stylish black hat was standing close by with an impatient grimace on her painted lips.

"Pardon me," Megan murmured and hastily stepped aside. The woman sailed past without another glance, the swish of silk skirts and the heady scent of French perfume lingering after her. Megan drew a quivering breath. She fought down the desire to turn around and escape to the anonymity of the street. Instead, she crossed the thick carpet to a chair.

Resolutely, she drew the newspaper ad from her handbag and read it for what must have been the hundredth time.

Industrious young woman needed to cook and

5

clean on a ranch in the Colorado Territory.
Between 20 and 25 years old. Orphan preferred.
Top wages. Inquire for Mr. Steven Chamberlin at
the Olympus Hotel.

The mended edge of her glove slipped from its hiding place beneath the sleeve of her jacket. Carefully, she tucked it back in.

Maybe Mr. Chamberlin has already found someone, she thought, mingling hope and fear. The ad had been published that morning, but she hadn't been able to get away from the shop until quite a while after lunch. Mrs. Peabody had grudgingly given her the last part of the afternoon off.

She noticed a distinguished gentleman who was sitting on a gold sofa reading a newspaper. Discreetly observing his features, she wondered again what Steven Chamberlin was like. Her mind drew a picture of a short man with a middle-aged paunch who smoked smelly, black cigars and had a booming voice. His wife, no doubt, was the kind who would be constantly peering over her shoulder and making clucking noises. She cringed inwardly and again stifled the urge to run away.

It was unthinkable that she, the daughter of a Virginia plantation owner, should be applying for a housekeeper's position. Her family had suffered many forms of humiliation through the last ten years, but nonetheless she was thankful her mother could not see her now.

It's a waste of time worrying about family pride, she reminded herself again. Jeremy, her little brother, was desperately ill, and the sanitarium was far beyond her means. If Jeremy was to get well, she had to have more money than she could earn at the dressmaker's shop.

The years since the War between the States had been a nightmare for Megan. The loss of her father and brother in the war, living in poverty in Baltimore, and her dear mother's death would have been enough to break the spirit of most girls.

How could they have survived without Em? Dear Em, who

had been with the family for more than twenty years. Em, who had stayed when the other freed slaves were sent away to find livings elsewhere. Thankfully, Em could watch over Jeremy if Megan had to leave.

Blinking, Megan held back the worried tears that blurred her vision. She drew the scrap of newsprint between two fingers, and the words "Top wages" caught her eye. She had to get this position.

A tall, dark-haired man slowly descending the wide staircase drew her attention. He scanned the lobby, pausing a moment at the foot of the stairs. Megan noticed his tailored black broadcloth suit, white silk shirt with tiny red pinstripes, and black string tie. He had broad shoulders and a square, purposeful chin.

Was that Steven Chamberlin? Her throat tightened when she realized he was striding in her direction.

"You were asking for Steven Chamberlin, ma'am?" he asked, bowing slightly. He spoke pleasantly enough, but his faint, polite smile didn't quite reach his eyes.

"Yes." Megan's tongue felt thick and uncooperative. "I came to apply for this position." She handed him the ad. Her hand was icy and shaking.

"I am Mr. Chamberlin." He sat in the chair facing her. "May I ask your qualifications?"

To her dismay she felt her cheeks growing hot. The speech she had rehearsed all morning flew beyond her reach. Frantically, she groped for it.

"I can cook and clean," she managed at last, then added with spirit, "and I can work as hard as anyone."

The young man took stock of her clothes, which were carefully made but showing signs of wear; the sweet, anxious mouth; the quiet courage in her eyes, and his manner softened slightly.

"What is your name?"

"Megan Wescott. I need employment badly. You see, my little brother is ill, and the sanitarium is expensive."

His wife would be about my own age, she thought, not sure if that was good or bad.

"Your parents?"

"Father was killed in the war, and Mother died five months ago." She met his gaze openly, candidly, and realized for the first time that his thick black eyebrows almost came together. "I've been working in a dressmaker's shop doing fine needlework, but with Jeremy sick I'll have to earn more."

"I'd like to talk to you about some details." He glanced around. The man she had observed shifted position and turned a page of his newspaper. Two men engrossed in conversation walked past. "Would you mind stepping into the hotel restaurant where we can talk more privately? There are some things I need to explain about the position."

"Will your wife join us?" Megan asked, confused.

"That's one of the things I'll need to explain," he said, standing.

Is his wife ill? A vague doubt sprouted in her mind.

An aloof waiter showed them to a small table in a back corner of the dining room. Megan allowed Mr. Chamberlin to seat her. She removed her gloves, clasped them tightly in her lap, and waited. Alive to his every expression, she tried to determine what lay behind the handsome, self-assured face across from her.

"It's quite a long story," he began after ordering coffee for two. "Two years ago, my father bought a four-hundred-acre ranch near Juniper Junction—that's about fifty miles north of Denver in the Colorado Territory—from a man who went back East. It's deeded land. I guess my father was planning to go there sometime, but he never did. He died a month ago, and left a small fortune to my sister and me. My mother died several years ago, you see.

"My half of the inheritance comes with a condition—my father's idea of giving me a test of character." His right eyebrow lifted slightly, giving him a vaguely cynical expression. He paused while the waiter set their coffee before them. "In order to inherit, my wife and I must live on the ranch for a full year and make it profitable."

"And you want a housekeeper for her?" Megan prompted. *Won't he ever come to the point?*

He added a spoonful of sugar to his coffee and stirred it thoughtfully. Megan watched the slow movement of his large, well-groomed hands. She looked up to find his measuring gaze upon her.

"I don't have a wife."

"I don't understand." *Maybe I ought to leave. This doesn't sound right.*

"I mean," he spoke slowly, distinctly, closely observing her reaction, "I'm looking for a housekeeper and cook who would be willing to become my legal wife for that year." He leaned forward, speaking softly. "I'll be frank. I could find a mail order bride if I wanted to. There are plenty of folks who are doing it these days. But I'm not ready to be saddled down with that responsibility. I wouldn't even go this far if it wasn't for losing a fortune in the process.

"After the terms of the will have been met, I'll have the marriage discreetly dissolved. No one in the East need ever know of the arrangement. I'm willing to pay one hundred dollars per month."

"But as your wife. . . ," Megan faltered. She struggled between dismay at his scheme and the knowledge that she desperately needed the amount of money he had quoted.

"A legality only, I assure you," he said. "Call it a make-believe marriage if that eases your conscience. I turned down two women this morning, but I think you and I could be partners. Why not? You need a sizable income, and I need a wife for a year. We can work together to accomplish both."

"But why would your father put your wife in his will if you aren't married?" *It didn't sound reasonable.*

"He thought I was," Mr. Chamberlin said, ruefully. "The last time I saw him was before the war. I was engaged at the time. What a foolish boy I was." He shook he head. "She was a hostess on the *Mississippi Queen*. I thought she cared for me, but she was only after my winnings at the poker table. She dumped me when a brighter star came along." His lips tightened. "I won't be so foolish again." He shrugged, and his expression softened. "Anyway, I didn't have any contact with my father after that visit. I guess he naturally assumed I had married."

"Couldn't you go to the solicitor and tell him you're not married?" Megan persisted, still puzzled.

"It would break the will." Again that hard look. "And Georgiana, my older sister, would dearly love to chisel me out of my half of the money." He leaned back in his chair and shook his head. "No. There's no other way."

Megan's slim fingers toyed with her china coffee cup. She stared at the painted yellow rose on the inside rim, weighing the possibilities. One hundred dollars a month was almost twice as much as she had hoped for. And what a relief not to have to please the tastes of another woman.

"What kind of work do you do?" She looked keenly at the man across from her. He didn't look unscrupulous, but there must be some reason his father hadn't trusted him.

Chamberlin laughed mirthlessly, gesturing with his hand.

"That's a good question, ma'am," he said, sobering. "It's right prudent of you to ask. I left home at sixteen and found out I could be handy with the pasteboards. That's the cards, ma'am. I rode the Mississippi riverboats for a few years, fought for the Confed'racy under Bragg, and then wandered around New Orleans after the war, trying my hand at this and that, gambling enough to keep me from starving.

"To tell you the truth, I was at a loss until this will came up. I think I'd like to have a go at ranching. Put down some roots, maybe." He shrugged. "At least I'd like to have a chance to prove I can do it even if I decide to come back East later. I don't have a predilection for the idea of marriage, that's all. I've been a loner for too long."

The simple directness of his answer convinced Megan he was being honest with her. There was a lengthy silence while she thought it over.

What would a meaningless marriage matter? Wasn't marriage a commitment of the heart? All he asked was what the ad said: a housekeeper and cook. It would be pleasant on a ranch, too. A ranch and a plantation were practically the same, weren't they? She remembered the corrals, the riding stable, the spreading lawn, and columned plantation house she had known as a child. The ranch would be different, of course, but there were similarities.

What a relief it would be to go back to that life even if she was only a servant.

But I won't be a servant, she suddenly recalled. *I would be the mistress.* Some of the cloud lifted from her mind. *Yes,* she rolled the idea around on her tongue, *I would be the mistress.*

"When would we have to leave?" she asked, slowly.

"Three weeks." He peered at her with half-closed eyes. "Does that mean you accept?"

"I can't see that I have any choice," she said, steadily. "Yes, I accept."

"Good." His expression relaxed. He reached inside his coat. "Here's my card. I'd like you to go to the Hurlick's General Store on Market Street and purchase any household goods you feel will be necessary. I'm afraid I wouldn't know where to begin when it comes to housekeeping, and I think it would be better for you to make your own choices. Give Hurlick this card, and he'll put it on my account. Have everything packed and sent to my address."

"What should I get?" Megan asked, taking the card and glancing at it.

"Whatever you'll need to take care of the house, and fix things up a mite. The house isn't large, I understand, but it has been empty for quite some time. Cooking utensils, curtains, and such like would be in order, I suppose."

Megan slid the card into her purse. Her hands were clammy, and she had the strange feeling she was somehow watching herself from far away.

"We can have the ceremony performed in a quiet corner of the city in about a week," he continued, "but I see no need to change our living quarters until we leave. If you need to contact me in the meantime, you can reach me here. How can I contact you?"

"I live at 148 High Street, Apartment 3B," she said. She pulled on her gloves and stood up. She wanted to have some time alone to adjust herself to the new circumstances.

"Thank you, Miss Wescott," he said, rising with her, the shadow of a smile on his lips.

"Megan," she said seriously. "It's foolish to continue formalities."

"Yes, Megan." He sobered. "I'm sure I don't need to tell you our arrangement shouldn't be known to anyone else. Will you meet me at the park near the big fountain with water spraying out a carp's mouth, say a week from today? At two o'clock?"

"I'll be there." She offered him her hand, and he clasped it briefly. His hand, though uncalloused, was surprisingly firm and strong. "Good day." With a nod, she left the hotel.

Conflicting emotions swept over her as she stepped, blinking, into the bright afternoon sunlight. A flush of exhilaration tingled through her as she mouthed the wage he had offered her. *A hundred dollars a month!* Her brightest hopes had never been audacious enough to rise up that high. The marriage contract was a little disturbing, but livable for a few months. However, now that she knew the problem of the sanitarium fee was solved, she had to face the dark side: leaving behind all she loved to brave the unknown. Many who ventured into the wild new territories were never heard from again.

A whole year. She was heartsick at the thought. *Can I do it? Can I say good-bye to Jeremy and Em?* She pushed back the walls that crowded in on her. She would not succumb to her fears and heartaches. If she caved in, Jeremy would sense it and be afraid, too. She must be strong for him.

She walked blindly along the cobblestone streets, unaware of the chilly May breeze that tickled her burning cheeks. Her feet beat a steady cadence on the sidewalk while she reminisced about the past and wondered about the future.

two

The years since the war were a series of murky shadows in Megan's memory. When the Southern Cause was lost, her family left Virginia and traveled north to Baltimore to stay with Mother's Aunt Alice. Daddy had fallen with a Yankee bullet in his chest. Silverleigh, their home, was a blackened heap of ash and rubble. Friends were scattered, never to be seen again. Gone forever was the world they had loved. They hoped to find rest and build a new life, but those hopes were shattered when Aunt Alice had a stroke and died. Debt swallowed her estate and again the Wescotts were homeless.

Mother was left without friend or advisor. It was up to her to provide a roof to cover their despairing heads and food to ease their gnawing stomachs. She walked the streets of the poorest, dirtiest section of Baltimore until she found an apartment, a dark, wretched cubbyhole, for a dollar a week. Intended for one or at the most two people, it had two closet-sized bedrooms barely big enough for a cot and a chair, a kitchen that was about the size of their dining room table at Silverleigh, and a sitting room that could be crossed in four strides from either direction.

The landlady, Mrs. Niles, looked Mother up and down as though mentally pricing every piece of clothing Mother wore before she grudgingly admitted she had a vacancy. She was a thin-lipped woman who had been middle-aged all her life. Her gown was a cheap imitation of the morning dresses that had filled two of Mother's closets at Silverleigh. However, the cut of the cloth was as far as the resemblance went; because the collar and cuffs were smudged, and there was a small tear under the arm, something Mother would never have permitted even in a servant. Though disgusted, Mother pretended not to notice and handed over the first week's rent, her last dollar but one, and in her mind playfully nicknamed the landlady Nilly-Willy. She made a joke of it to the children later that evening.

What it must have cost Mother's aristocratic pride to knock on door after door asking women if she could do their washing and ironing. The family lived on bread and tea the first few weeks they lived at Mrs. Niles's tenement house. Finally, the news of Mother's and Em's excellent work with soapsuds, starch, and hot iron traveled across the grapevine of Baltimore's housewives, and the amount of work grew until they had money to buy enough food to satisfy a growing boy and, of course, pay their rent.

Mother insisted that Megan, scarcely more than a child, continue her schooling. She found a church with a mission that taught slum children and made Megan attend the classes. Mother filled the gaps in their meager program by teaching Megan by lamplight after a twelve-hour day of bending over a scrub board or iron.

Megan watched her mother's soft, white hands become red and coarse from hours in hot, soapy water. She knew Mother would never allow a word of complaint to pass her lips, and she would not allow anyone else to grumble, either. She never let it be spoken, but she could not hide her suffering, worry-filled eyes.

How could they have made it without Em? Always near with a strong back and willing, loving hands, Em comforted them and offered her earthy wisdom to chase away discouragement.

Years of brutal work and the lack of fresh air broke down Mother's health. She grew weaker and weaker until she had a fainting spell over the wash tub. Unable to hide their tears, Megan and Em lifted Mother to her tiny cot, brought her hot broth, and tried to make her comfortable. There was no money for a doctor.

Megan stopped going to school. Instead, she took Mother's place in the soapsuds until Mother, broken in spirit and body, called Megan to her side a few months before she died. Mother's smooth, clear face now had deep creases around the eyes and mouth. In two months' time her hair had turned the color of moonlight reflected on new-fallen snow.

"I want you to get a position in the city, Megan," she wheezed, stopping often to take a breath. Her translucent hand reached out to touch Megan's cheek. "You'll ruin yourself with this backbreaking work. It's not fittin' for a pretty young thing like you to spend her life with her hands in wash water."

How courageous Mother had been through all their struggle, never thinking of herself, always thinking of Megan and Jeremy.

&

Cold hard emptiness had filled the apartment when Mother was taken from them. The burning ache was still fresh in Megan's bosom.

Following Mother's advice, Megan took samples of her work and applied at a shop close to the center of town. She had learned to weave lace and sew fine embroidery from her governess, who had considered it a necessity for a young lady destined to join the higher ranks of society. Megan was an artist with her needle, and she loved her work. At her first stop, Mrs. Peabody, the owner of the dressmaker's shop, had hired her instantly when Megan had spread out her handiwork.

It had been enjoyable to sit in the back room of the shop and handle the beautiful threads. However, the sense of enjoyment lasted only a few months. Mother's death squeezed the last ounce of joy out of Megan's life, and when Jeremy contracted rheumatic fever a few months later, Megan felt desperation grip her. The responsibility weighed her down until she felt she would smother.

&

The light was beginning to fade when Megan at last set a course for home. She reached her neighborhood with her thoughts still far off. Habitually stepping around bits of broken glass and refuse, she walked on. She didn't notice the thin children huddled together in doorways and on the front steps of their homes or the starving mongrel dogs sniffing the gutters for a morsel of decaying food. When she reached High Street she stepped off the crumbling sidewalk to pass a group of ragged boys playing marbles on the corner.

" 'Lo, Megan," one urchin called.

"Hello, Joe." She smiled absently in response and walked on.

Suddenly, the chance to leave the city gave her a new awareness of her neighborhood. She awoke from her sleepwalking and looked around at the soot-covered buildings and trash-laden street. The acrid smell of unwashed bodies and rotting garbage pricked her nose. In the depths of the building nearby a man and woman raised their voices in a heated argument, while a baby wailed relentlessly. High Street had never seemed so dismal as today, the tenement houses never so dirty and depressing.

How wonderful it would be to get away from the city. To breathe fresh air, to feel free-blowing breezes in her hair, the sun on her face. To see wide, unbounded country crowned with a clear, sapphire sky.

The soothing smell of Em's thick stew welcomed Megan when she opened the apartment door. She was pulling off her gloves, adjusting her eyes to the dimness, when a tall, lean black woman came to stand in the kitchen doorway. She wore a faded gingham dress with a white apron. Her gray hair was pulled back from her face, seamed by years of hard work and sorrow. She held a dish towel in her hands.

"How is Jeremy, Em?"

"Sleepin'. I gave him some supper 'bout an hour ago." Em peered at Megan, her narrow face creased with worry. "Did you find you a new job, Miss Megan?"

"Yes, I did." Megan removed her bonnet and laid it on the shelf near the door. Hanging her jacket on a peg, she followed Em into the tiny kitchen wondering how to tell her the rest of the news. Saying it aloud made their separation seem more real. "It pays almost twice as much as I had hoped for, Em," she said, slowly, "but there is something I didn't tell you about."

"What do you have to do?" Em asked, anxiously.

"I'm keeping house and cooking like I told you. . . ," Megan paused, avoiding Em's eyes. "But I have to go out to the Colorado Territory."

"The Colorado Territory! Lord have mercy, child, whatever for?" She stared at Megan, her lips slightly parted. The dimple in her right cheek, the one Megan called her worry mark, deepened as Megan continued.

"The gentleman has a ranch out there, and he needs a housekeeper. I've agreed to go for a year," Megan said, softly.

"A year!" Two tears slid slowly down Em's anguished face, and Megan felt her resolve bubbling away.

"Please don't cry, Em," she begged, putting arms around Em, her face on Em's shoulder. "I don't want to go. You know I don't." The tears she had been battling all afternoon finally won out. In a moment she drew back, wiping her eyes. "I have no choice. You see that, don't you?"

"Yes, child." Em's seamed, careworn face was wet also. "I know." She sank into a chair with a heavy sigh, her face a picture of misery. "It's the lonesome days ahead I'm a-thinkin' on."

"I'll make enough money so you won't have to work so hard." Megan knelt by Em's side and clasped her bony, work-hardened hands between her own. "If we can find you a place in a rooming house near the sanitarium, you can visit Jeremy every day. And you can get away from this dark, crowded tenement house. It will be better for us all." She searched Em's face for a sign of comfort.

"When you leavin'?"

"In three weeks. We have so much to do before then. I'll have to keep my job with Mrs. Peabody for another week or so. We'll have to make arrangements with the sanitarium and find you a place to stay." She looked around the kitchen. "We'll have to pack all our things, too."

"Em!" A faint call came from the bedroom.

"I'll go to Jeremy," Megan said, rising. She gave Em's hand a squeeze and ran to wash away the traces of tears.

The coal oil lamp Megan carried into Jeremy's bedroom cast a golden light over the child's hollow cheeks. His skin was almost transparent, his lips tinged a faint blue. His large night-shirt made him seem smaller than his ten years. Tousled, straw-colored hair came down to his eyes, now sunken and dulled by weeks of illness. His languid expression faded a little when he realized who it was that carried the lamp.

"How is my little soldier?" Megan asked, smiling tenderly. She set the lamp on the small table beside a chipped enamel basin. The splash of lamplight touched both walls in the narrow room.

"Megan," Jeremy murmured, a drowsy smile on his lips. "I'm glad you're home. Can you stay with me for a little while?"

"I'll stay with you as long as you like." She plumped his pillow, and straightened the counterpane. "I have some grown-up business to talk over with you tonight."

"What is it?" His tired eyes showed a spark of curiosity.

"Well, part of it is good, and part of it is kind of hard." She eased into the straight wooden chair by his bed. "You know what the doctor said about having to take special care of you to protect your heart?"

"Sure," he said impatiently. "That's why I have to stay in this old bed all day long."

"Today I found work that will make it possible for you to get the treatments you need to get better."

"You did?"

"Yes. I'm going next week to make the arrangements with the doctor." She hesitated, dreading the rest of her news.

"What's the hard part?" He tried to sit up by supporting himself on his elbows. "Don't worry, Meg. I can take it. I'm no baby. Did the doctor tell you something bad about me?"

"Oh, no, Jeremy," she assured him quickly. "Don't even think such a thing. He said with proper care he has good hopes you'll soon be well." She pressed her bottom lip between her teeth. "It's that the job I found is far away in Colorado. I'm going to be a housekeeper on a ranch."

"Is Em going, too?" His voice had a touch of anxiety.

"Of course not. Em will stay near you and come to visit you every day. We wouldn't leave you all alone."

"Long as Em's with me I won't mind." He lay back against the pillow, his restless hands feeling the texture of the nubby counterpane. He lay still a moment, absorbing the news until a new idea struck him. "Out West?" He raised himself on one arm again and looked more boyish than before. "Will there be Injuns and rustlers and everything?"

"I don't think so," Megan said, smiling gently. "There will be horses, though, like we had in Virginia. But what I wanted to tell you," she went on, "is that I'll have to stay there a year."

"Do you think I could go, too, when I get better?" he pleaded.

"I don't know, dear. We'll have to see." Dismayed by his flushed face and his quick, shallow breathing, she warned, "Don't get too wrought up. You must stay quiet."

"Wow, cowboys and everything!" he whispered. Reluctantly, he relaxed against the pillow. His eyes closed for a moment, then flew open to seek Megan's face in the dim light. "I'll try hard to get better, Meg, so I can come out and be with you."

She turned the lamp lower and whispered the platitudes she hoped would calm him, thankful he couldn't see her tears through the shadows. When he was dozing she padded softly back to Em in the kitchen.

"He took it like my soldier boy," she told Em who was dishing up two bowls of stew. "He wants to come out to see the Indians and the rustlers when he gets well." She filled a thick, white mug from the metal water pitcher on the table and sipped it.

"That boy's a reg'lar angel." Em shook her head, smiling sadly. "I'll take care o' him, Miss Megan. Don't you grieve yourself 'bout that."

The next week was emotionally exhausting for Megan. Like a saber-wielding duelist she beat back her fears. Her head knew that going away with Steve Chamberlin was the only answer to her predicament, but her heart moaned in torment. Each evening as she sat with Jeremy, white-hot daggers pierced her through.

I can't do it, she'd despair. *You must,* she'd argue back. *You must. You must.*

The nights she spent tossing fitfully on her hard, narrow cot. The days found her working her usual ten hours at the dressmaker's shop, making lists of things to do and take, and sorting their few possessions. The night before the wedding she didn't close her eyes until the faint gray light of dawn crept wearily through her tiny window.

three

The next morning was as tedious and long as the morning at Silverleigh when Megan broke Mother's favorite china figurine while her parents were away. She had spent four dreadful, restless hours waiting for them to return and discover her guilt. Like then, Megan couldn't concentrate on anything else except the dreaded event. This time it was her appointment with Steve Chamberlin that overshadowed all else.

She had asked Mrs. Peabody for the day off but when the day arrived she wished she had asked for only the afternoon, because her job would have filled the empty morning hours. Instead, she had to pass the time wandering from room to room, looking out windows, sitting down with a book only to put it aside five minutes later with barely a line read. She absently straightened pillows and ran errands for Jeremy. At ten-thirty she lay on her cot, feeling tired after her sleepless night and hopped up in two minutes to continue pacing. Her taut muscles must keep moving. She could not think of closing her eyes.

After forcing down three bites of lunch, she took her time changing into her best dress, a pale lavender cotton with a faint ivory swirl woven into it. She parted her waist-length hair slightly right of center and pulled it back into a wide, brown bun at the nape of the neck. Putting on her navy bonnet and coat, she left the house early to walk off some of her nervous energy.

There was a chill in the air when she reached the street. The sky over the city was dotted with small, puffy clouds, and a warm, fitful breeze toyed with the strings of her bonnet. Without any haste, she headed in the general direction of the park

Steve had mentioned. She still had an hour to wait and the walk would normally take only twenty minutes.

The park, carpeted with a freshly grown crop of young grass and trees tinged with waxy, yellow-green new leaves, was almost deserted when she arrived. Mothers had their tiny charges at home for naps while older children were still in school. Megan wandered aimlessly on the path near a duck pond until she found a perch on a bench near the fish fountain Steve had told her about. With a detached attitude, she watched three mallard ducks dive for bread crumbs thrown by a grizzled old man in a tattered felt hat. Across the path a clump of daffodils swayed in the occasional breeze, bobbing their heads toward Megan.

Can I really go through with it? The question that had been battering her mind for the past week reverberated again in full force. She suddenly realized she was clenching her teeth, and she tried to force herself to relax.

Sunshine spilled over her back, slowly warming and loosening her tense muscles. Her lack of sleep from the night before took its toll, and little by little she began to feel drowsy. Her eyes were drooping when the old man with the bread crumbs carefully folded his empty sack and put it into the pocket of his faded, blue overcoat. He lingered a few moments longer before stomping down the path out of the park. Megan's gaze idly followed him until she saw something that roused her from her lethargy.

With a gray derby pulled low over his forehead, Steve Chamberlin strode past the old man, looking left then right as he came. He was dressed all in gray from overcoat to leather shoes. His face cleared when he spotted Megan, and he closed the gap between them in seconds.

"You came!" He settled down beside her. "I had almost convinced myself you would change your mind." The indecision on Megan's face stopped him. He looked at her carefully. "You're still going to do it, aren't you?"

"I can't afford to change my mind," she answered hesitantly. Seeing him again had brought a rush of panic over her.

"How is your brother?" he asked, politely.

"He's about the same, thank you." She studied the tiny stitches on the back of her gloved hand lying in her lap. Her own words echoed in her mind. Jeremy was the same, and he wouldn't get better unless she fulfilled her duty to him. When the full impact of that realization came to her, her pulse quieted. The confused, troubled thoughts fell into order.

"Did you find a sanitarium?"

"Yes. There's one on the western edge of town on Oak Street called Pinefield Nursing Home. They have an open bed and can take Jeremy as soon as I bring the first month's fee."

"We'll take care of that today. After the wedding, we'll visit my solicitor and make all the arrangements."

She rose, and they strolled to a closed carriage waiting nearby. Steve curtly called out an address to the driver, handed Megan up, and they set off at a brisk trot. Megan clasped her purse in her lap and kept her attention on the scene passing before the side window of the carriage. She felt too wrought up inside to take part in small talk. Evidently, Chamberlin either sensed or shared her mood, because he was silent for the entire journey.

The wedding was cold and mechanical. Without raising his head, a white-haired preacher read the solemn words from a small black book, his stout, red-cheeked wife looking on. Steve slid a plain gold band on her finger, and it was over. Megan's hands trembled, and she felt chilled clear through, yet she felt a bit lighter, a trifle less burdened. She breathed a deep, silent sigh. There was no turning back now. Her future was sealed.

The wedding was followed by an uncomfortable trip to Cyrus Tump's, the solicitor's office, where Steve introduced Megan and notified the ancient, spectacled gentleman of their plan to move to Colorado. Megan was afraid the steely, gray eyes of the lawyer would bore right through her, but she resolutely met his gaze and even managed a smile and nod in response to his greeting. Steve made arrangements for Jeremy's sanitarium fee and a monthly allowance for Em to be paid from Mr. Tump's office.

Back in the waiting carriage, he handed her a white envelope. "This is your first two months' pay."

"Thank you." She put the envelope in her handbag, then slid the gold band from her finger and placed it carefully into an inside pocket of the handbag for safekeeping.

"Is there any way I can help you?" he offered kindly when she pulled the drawstring tight.

"Em needs a small place to stay near the sanitarium so she can be near Jeremy. We haven't been able to find anything yet."

"I'll see to it," he said easily, and wrote it down in a small notebook he withdrew from his pocket.

"When exactly are we leaving?"

"That would be May twenty-fifth at six-thirty in the morning. We travel to Chicago, then change trains and go on to Denver. It'll take about a week."

"Only a week to go so far?" She had expected him to say twice as long.

"I want to get there in time to plant some corn, so it's none too fast. We'd leave this week if I could have gotten tickets." He returned the pad to his pocket. "Can I see you home?"

"Well, I was going to make the arrangements at the sanitarium for Jeremy...."

"I'll take you there, then." He gave the order to the driver. "I don't have anything pressing this afternoon," he said, settling back on the black leather seat.

Megan was buoyed up with relief when Steve left her on High Street later that afternoon. A place in the sanitarium had been secured and a carriage engaged for Jeremy's transfer there. It was beyond marvelous to know that skilled hands would be caring for him tomorrow.

❧

The next two weeks were a blur of activity. Megan and Em packed their few belongings and scrubbed the apartment. They were leaving it far cleaner than they had found it. It was heart-breaking to go through Mother's things, a task she had shied away from thus far. Mourning was momentarily replaced by excitement when she found some forgotten treasures in an old trunk. There was the forest green riding habit that had been Father's last gift to Mother before the war. She tried it on and found that with a few alterations she could wear it.

She hesitated when she found Father's old Bible, wrapped carefully in black velvet and brown paper. Never read, it had been kept by Mother as a momento. Reverently, Megan un-wrapped it and ran her fingers gently over the black leather cover. Replacing the wrapping, she put it with the rest of her treasures. It would be comforting to have a few familiar things with her when she was far away.

Shopping was exhausting but also exciting. She bought blankets, feather ticking, coal oil lamps, vegetable seeds, a large cast-iron pot, needles, thread, several bolts of gaily colored fabric in check and small prints, and many other things.

She tried to concentrate totally on the task of clearing out the apartment and getting ready to go, pushing thoughts of good-byes far into the back recesses of her mind. The twenty-fourth of May soon arrived, however, and she could ignore good-byes no longer. She visited Jeremy that afternoon as she did every afternoon. Only, today it was with a sinking spirit.

At the door of the ward, she hesitated on the threshold to see what he was doing before she came closer. His eyes closed, Jeremy seemed to be asleep. Megan tiptoed toward him, study-ing his face, savoring the sight of him. In spite of the fact that she had not made a sound, his eyelids fluttered when she reached his side. Slowly, he focused on her.

"Hello, Meg."

"How are you feeling, Jeremy?" She pushed his hair back from his forehead, letting her hand rest near his temple.

" 'Bout the same." He paused, gazing listlessly at her face. "It's tomorrow, isn't it?"

"I'm afraid it is," Megan whispered, suddenly choked. A powerful hand gripped the core of her being. "I'm leaving in the morning."

"I'm going to miss you, Meg." A single, lonely tear slid slowly down his pale cheek. Megan gathered him in her arms and held him close. She shut her eyes hard, squeezing back the tears.

"Be my soldier, Jeremy," she said, forcing calmness into her words. "While I'm working in Colorado, you work hard on getting well. I'll try to send for you when you're better. I promise." She lay him back on the pillow and gently wiped away his tears with her handkerchief. "You keep remembering those horses and cowboys you want to see so bad, okay?" She attempted a bright smile through stiff lips.

"I will," he said bravely. His lip quivered, but he didn't cry anymore. His fingers clutched at her hand. "Will you write to me?"

"Of course. You don't think I'd forget about my best beau, do you?" she asked, lightly. "I'll write so much you'll get tired of reading."

"I'll get better as hard as I can," he promised solemnly.

"One day this will all be past, and we'll be happy again," she said softly, "but until then we'll both have to be good soldiers." She held his hand to her lips. "Always remember I love you."

"I love you, too, Meg." His lip quivered again. "Don't worry. Em will look after me."

Gently, she kissed his cheek, hugged him, and whispered a good-bye in his ear. She left the room without looking back. She couldn't endure the sight of him small and ill and alone, looking after her. But not looking back wasn't the answer, for the image of Jeremy in the sickbed was branded into her mind.

Tears coursed down her cheeks. She pressed her handkerchief to her mouth to stifle wracking sobs. Outside the door of the ward she leaned a shoulder against the cool wall, trying to get composure. In vain she drew in huge gulps of air and squeezed her sodden handkerchief tightly to her burning eyes. Finally, with tears still flowing, she straightened her shoulders, lifted her chin, and walked on.

❧

The next morning, Megan and Em rose while it was still dark to get ready for Megan's departure. The apartment had a strange, hollow quality that echoed and amplified their voices and the little noises of their moving about. Megan's trunk stood, locked and ready, near the front door. Em's was in the middle of the living room. Em would finish the transfer of her things later that morning and return the key to Mrs. Niles.

Megan couldn't swallow a bite of food. Though Em pressed her, she could force down only a few sips of hot coffee. After placing a few final things in her case, she walked through the apartment one last time to check for anything forgotten. Her shoes made a resonating clump-clump sound on the bare wood floors. The faint light of day glimmered through the curtainless windows, making vague patterns on the walls and floor.

Memories swept over her during her stroll from room to room. In this remote, dark place she had laughed and wept these past eight years. Her mother had died here. Here she had grown to womanhood.

She stared sightlessly down at the street, hazy in the new dawn, until she felt Em's hand on her arm.

"He's a-comin' soon, Miss Megan."

"I know." Megan looked up into Em's sad face. The worry mark was deep. "Oh, Em!" Her courage wavered for an instant.

"Just take it one day at a time, Miss Megan," Em said, putting a strong, loving arm around her. "That's the only way to git through the hard times. I seen a-plenty, but they always pass, child. They always pass."

The clip-clop of hooves and the squeal of iron rims on cobblestones sounded below.

"He's here." Dread put an edge on Megan's voice. She hugged Em hard and a few tears spilled over. "I'll send a telegram when we arrive."

"You in the hands o' the good Lord, Miss Megan. If prayin' ever helped anybody, you be all right, 'cause I'll sure enough be a-prayin'." Tears flowed down her dark, wrinkled cheeks.

A light tap sounded at the door. Trying futilely to dry her eyes, Megan opened it. It took but a moment for Steve's man to remove the trunk, and Steve took the case.

Moving mechanically, Megan put on her bonnet and coat against the chilly morning air. She took a step toward the door, then paused. With a sob, she threw herself into Em's arms, squeezing her hard, then she tore herself away and ran down the stairs, her heels beating a staccato tempo in her haste.

When she thought back later, all she could remember of the trip to the train station was a blur of impressions: the clop-clop of the horses pulling the carriage, the soft, steady pressure of Steve's hand on her arm guiding her through the waiting crowd, the aroma of cigar smoke in the passenger car, her wet cheeks and puffy, burning eyes.

They were in their seats less than five minutes before the train lurched ahead with a chugg-chugg-chugg that grew into a throbbing clackety-clack as it gathered speed. The sound pounded in Megan's tortured brain until it rang in her ears: *You're-not-coming-back. You're-not-coming-back.* She rested her head against the high back of the red plush seat and turned toward the window. The exhaustion of the past three weeks washed over her. The sound and sway of the train lulled her anguished mind until she fell asleep.

❧

It was near noon when next she opened her eyes. She blinked against the glare of the sun streaming through the train window and dazedly looked around. For a long second she couldn't remember where she was. It was Steve, beside her, reading a newspaper that brought her to herself. Catching a glimpse of herself in the gleaming mirror between the windows, she reached up to straighten her bonnet. She felt scruffy and had a nagging ache in her shoulder.

"Good morning," Steve said, smiling pleasantly, "though I believe it's closer to noon." He looked at her closer, realizing her discomfort. "There's a powder room near the back of the car if you'd like to refresh yourself."

"I believe I will," she said, picking up her handbag from where it had slid into the corner beside her. She avoided Steve's gaze as she passed by him, and half-stumbled down the aisle of the pitching, swaying car.

Megan bathed her red, swollen eyes and smoothed her hair back into its thick, brown bun. The cool water revived her somewhat and cleared her muddled mind. Taking advantage of the privacy, she placed the gold wedding band on her finger, this time to stay. Light though it was, it weighed heavily on her hand. She could feel it even when she replaced her glove.

On the return trip, she braced herself by holding the backs of the seats and noticed for the first time how crowded the car was. Two fat businessmen, one puffing a long, black cigar, were deep in conversation. Several coatless young men in silk pinstriped shirts with black sleeve garters were engaged in some sort of card game near the front of the car, shrilly encouraged by three gaudy young women with rouge-reddened cheeks. A fine lady in a black satin traveling suit sat alone near a window, waving a tiny square of black lace in front of her nose. Megan felt particular sympathy for the mothers. There were several of them with fussing, wriggling children. With the exception of the one next to the woman in black, every seat was occupied.

The sound of many voices, the mechanical noises of the train, and the smell of box lunches, tobacco smoke, and sickly sweet perfume filled the air.

"Care for some lunch?" Steve asked, reaching under the seat for the box he had brought.

"I couldn't." Her stomach was a leaden knot.

"You'll be sick if you don't eat." He watched her thoughtfully.

"You must think I'm a crybaby," she ventured impulsively.

"On the contrary. I believe I could be a little jealous."

Surprised, she glanced at him to see if he was mocking her, but his face was serious. He met her eyes.

"When I left, no one noticed in the least," he added, soberly. "No one has noticed for a long time." He broke the mood by studying the contents of their lunch box. "There's cold chicken, rolls, a piece of cheese, and a bottle of water and two cups. Surely you can take something."

"I guess I could take a roll," she yielded, holding out her hand. She was surprised at how good it tasted after she got past the first bite.

Grassy, rolling meadows skimpily dotted with horses and cattle skimmed past the window. Megan drank in each scene. She had been in the city for so long she had almost forgotten how lovely the countryside could be.

"How long until we reach Chicago?"

"About three days. Give or take a day." He handed her a cup of water. "We'll stop for dinner in Philadelphia, then on to Ohio and Chicago. There's an overnight stay in Chicago before we can get a train to Denver."

Hour by endless hour the journey stretched on. It seemed to Megan she was in limbo. Nothing existed but the clackety-clack of the train, the continuous pain in her heart, and Steve.

four

The stagecoach waiting for them in Denver was brilliant red with shiny gold trim. Over its double doors the name *Concord* glowed proudly. Megan was surprised to see that even the wheel rims were scarlet. The team of four sleek, black horses jangled the harness impatiently.

So this is the great West, Megan thought, hungrily absorbing every detail. Men in cowboy garb were lounging at various storefronts, engaged in desultory conversation. Now and then one would break away and amble down the boardwalk, six-shooter swinging, chaps flapping with each long stride. The women were dressed much more simply than those in Baltimore. Calico and homespun were everywhere.

Some of her self-consciousness had faded during the eight-day trip to Denver. Steve was casual and kind. She found soothing support in his presence. In Chicago, there had been an embarrassed silence when they reached their hotel suite, but he had arranged his blankets in the outer room and had given Megan privacy. Only twice did she have to hide tears of homesickness, though her thoughts strayed often to Jeremy and Em.

She felt a thrill of anticipation when Steve handed her up into the stage. In a few hours she would see her new home and begin her new life. What would it be like?

As soon as the stage pulled away from the broad streets of Denver, the rough, country road jarred Megan to the core. Her already-aching muscles begged for relief but the hard leather seats were unrelenting. The four other passengers, three men and one woman, exchanged introductions with Steve.

"Coming for a visit?" asked the stout, talkative woman known as Mrs. Pleurd.

"We're going to settle on the Cunningham place," Steve said, steadying himself by holding the edge of the seat.

"The Circle C?" blurted Mrs. Pleurd. Her mouth dropped open for half an instant before she recovered herself.

All of a sudden every eye was fastened on Steve. There was an uneasy silence.

"Why, yes," Steve said, lightly. "My father bought the land about two years ago, and I've come to take possession."

No one offered any more conversation, but Megan could sense the strain. Something in these otherwise friendly people was amiss. Was it something Steve had said or done? Megan probed her mind for an answer, but none came.

The shallow, winding stream where the driver chose to stop for lunch was peaceful and cool. Megan moved apart from the rest of the party to sit in the shade of a wide cottonwood tree, her back resting against its broad, steady trunk. She closed her eyes, breathing deeply of the clear air and resting her mind in the quietness while Steve went to the stream for some water.

In a few moments, hushed voices jarred her to full attention. She sat still, her head tilted to one side, listening to Steve's voice.

"I'm much obliged for your concern, Kip," Steve was saying to the man who had introduced himself as the foreman of the Running M, "but we'll go ahead with our plans."

"I'm just thinking of the little lady," a deep voice said. "Them Harringtons are plumb mean, and you'll have yourself a whoppin' fight. I hope you know what you're doing."

"I know." Steve's voice had a deadly, still quality. "I've been down the river a ways myself. We'll go on."

The snap of a boot on a twig told Megan they had moved away. She relaxed against the rough bark once more, but the memory of those voices lingered on, and her peace of mind flew away on silent wings.

A hot, lazy June afternoon gave them a drowsy welcome when the stage rumbled into Juniper Junction. From under the brim of her gray traveling bonnet, Megan eagerly watched the town roll by. The street was deserted except for three sleepy horses standing three-legged next to various hitching rails along the dusty street and two weather-beaten wagons. At various places a tepid breeze blew the sand into a small, swirling cloud.

"Whoa!" the driver bellowed as the stage lumbered to a halt. The clamor of the jouncing, jolting stage still sang in Megan's ears, and her stiff muscles complained when Steve helped her down. She stepped up onto the boardwalk and looked with interest at the shops and houses. There were one, two, yes, three saloons, and two blacksmith shops, a hotel, a bank, and a general store, as well as the stage station where she stood. Someone was building a small shop between the livery stable and the jail. It was a lonely place even compared to Denver, and wouldn't bear comparing to the crowded, pulsating streets of Baltimore.

Brushing aside a tinge of disappointment at the forsaken little place that would be their main supply point, Megan entered the stage station to send Em a telegram and ask if a letter had arrived.

"Sorry, ma'am." The boyish clerk with pock-scarred cheeks shook his head. "The mail comes through ever' Wednesday. Maybe there'll be somethin' tomorrow."

Twenty minutes later Megan sank gratefully into the wooden chair Steve held for her at the hotel restaurant. He looked anxiously at her weary face when he took his seat across from her at the small, square table.

"Do you think we should wait until morning to go on?" he asked.

"A little rest and some hot food is all I need," she replied, trying to smile. "I want to get to the ranch today. I don't think I could wake up and face another day of traveling." In her mind she pictured the wide fields and spreading trees on the ranch. She could already feel the long, refreshing bath and the bed waiting for her there.

Two thick steaks and a plateful of fried potatoes later they walked outside to see four horses hitched to a buckboard in front of the general store next door. In the wagon were their suitcases and baggage.

"Aren't they beauties?" Steve asked, a hint of pride in the words.

"Where did you find them?" Holding his arm, she stopped on the edge of the boardwalk, looking eagerly at each horse in turn. There were two blacks, a buckskin, and a strawberry roan mare.

"Man at the livery stable had the three geldings and the buckboard. I got the mare from Harper at Harper's Emporium."

Megan rubbed the neck of the strawberry mare. Memories of happy days in Virginia came back in a flood. Morning rides with Father, all but forgotten, were revived again. The mare nuzzled her hand.

"Looking for a treat?" Megan laughed happily and patted the star between the horse's eyes. "What's her name?"

"Candy. Harper tells me she loves sugar and carrots. His daughter had her until she went back East. Treated her like a baby. She married a man from Delaware a few months ago, so Harper has no need to keep the horse around anymore." He checked a strap on the harness. "The black with the star and three stockings is Star, the one with the blaze is Caesar, and the buckskin is Billy."

"Will it take four to pull the buckboard?"

"It's a steep climb to the ranch from what I hear. When the wagon is loaded down like it is now, we'll be glad to have four." Steve finished his inspection of the harness. "We'd better get our supplies and head out." He pulled his watch from his vest pocket and glanced at it. "Billy has a loose shoe that must be attended to before we set out, and we ought to get to the ranch before dark."

It was shadowy inside Harper's Emporium after the glare of the hot afternoon sun. Megan paused on the threshold while she waited for her eyes to adjust to the dimness. The inviting aroma of new leather, fresh ground coffee, and tobacco drew her inside. From that moment, the smell of a new saddle reminded her of Harper's.

In one corner on a table were two saddles with some bridles and spurs; a few leather belts hung on the wall above them. There were large, copper-banded barrels of pickles, crackers, and coffee beans near the end of the counter where the coffee grinder stood. The rows of shelves that lined the wall behind the counter were filled with bolts of fabric, shirts and pants folded in a neat stack, an assortment of guns and ammunition, and various staple food items. On the counter was a thick glass jar of peppermint candy with a small sign: PENNY CANDY.

"Hello." A slim young woman standing near the counter spoke to Megan. Her strawberry blond hair was pulled back into a wavy, shoulder-length ponytail. "Mr. Harper went into the back room for a minute." She had clear blue eyes, and an open, friendly smile. "I'm Susan Harrington."

"I'm Megan Wes. . .ummm, Megan Chamberlin," Megan faltered. "We came in on the stage."

"Are you going to be here long?" The woman's friendliness touched Megan's heart and made her want to reach out.

"We've come to settle on a ranch."

"Oh, good!" Susan's smile broadened. "Elaine Sanders and I are about the only young women near Juniper since Alice Harper left. Where are you going to be?"

"I believe it's called the Circle C."

Her pleasant expression froze on Susan's face. She grew pale, and her eyes opened wide.

"The Circle C?" She paused, searching Megan's face.

"Yes. I hope you'll come and visit me if you can," Megan said, offering a tremulous smile. She hoped Susan would be a friend in this friendless, faraway place.

"I will." A spark shone in the local woman's eyes. She glanced toward the curtained doorway at the rear of the shop. The noise of boots scuffling on the wood floor came from the other side of the curtain. Susan moved closer to Megan. "I will come and visit you," she hurriedly whispered on her way out.

A slim, gray-haired man with stooped shoulders stepped through the curtain-covered door.

"Can I help you folks?"

"We need supplies." Steve spoke from the corner near the leather goods. "My wife can tell you what she wants."

Megan walked to the counter. "Twenty pounds of flour, two pounds of brown sugar. . . ." She gave Mr. Harper the list of supplies, enough for a month.

"I want five hundred rounds of .45 shells and five hundred .44s," Steve added when she finished. "And I'll take those two Colts, a Winchester, and the Henry rifle." He nodded toward weapons on a shelf to the left.

Harper's bushy, gray eyebrows raised a mite. He dropped the shells into the burlap sack he was filling.

"Expectin' trouble?" he asked, his eyes still on the sack.

"We've come to settle on the Circle C," Steve said, conversationally, "and we aim to stay."

Harper looked up, startled, to meet Steve's gaze for a long moment. The storekeeper's eyes shifted, and he continued filling their order in silence.

"I'll be needing a hand."

"You'll not be finding one for the Circle C," Mr. Harper said. His face was expressionless.

"Mr. Harper, I'm not on the prod, but if a fight comes my way, I'll handle it. With or without a hand." Steve lifted a burlap sack in each hand and carried them outside. Megan followed him, her heart pounding.

"I saw a blacksmith at work near the end of the street," Steve said, picking up the reins. "He ought to be able to take care of Billy's loose shoe in short order."

The pounding of a hammer on an anvil reached Megan's ears long before she saw the giant of a man who wielded the iron. He stood inside the wide open door of his shop, shaping a red-hot horseshoe. His bulging, hairy arms were streaked with soot and sweat. When their buckboard creaked to a stop he straightened, lifted the horseshoe with a pair of tongs, and plunged it into a bucket of water, making it boil over.

He was the biggest man Megan had ever seen. At least six-feet, four-inches tall, he must have weighed close to three hundred pounds. He wore a ragged shirt, so faded and dirty that it was impossible to tell its original color. Wide suspenders made two furrows over his shoulders, and his front was covered by a blackened leather apron.

"Gud afternoon!" Nodding and wiping his hands on his apron, he lumbered toward them. His broad grin revealed a missing front tooth.

Setting the brake and winding the reins around the whip stand, Steve jumped down. "I've got a horse with a loose shoe. Can you take care of it for me right away? We have some traveling to do before nightfall."

"Five minute," the blacksmith announced in thick, German tones. He picked up Billy's foot and examined the shoe. "Two nail vill make it gud as new." He slid a hammer from a loop on his side and dug two nails from his apron pocket. Four taps and he slid the hammer back through its loop. "I never seen you before. You live here?" It was a friendly question.

"We're settling on the Circle C." Steve's voice had become defensive.

"Dat's gud. Dat's gud." The big man's round, blond head bobbed up and down. "I'm Logan Hohner. I have de Horseshoe Ranch

just north of dere. Dose be my two boys, Al and Henry." He
indicated two young men in their early twenties slouching in
wooden chairs in front of the gray, wind-scoured building. At
the mention of their names, the one with buckteeth protruding
through his lips raised his hat a fraction then slid it over his
eyes and tilted back in his chair. The other nodded sullenly.
Both were of large build like their father except the father was
hard and muscular, and they were soft and lethargic.

"Come by my place any time," Hohner invited.

Steve thanked him and climbed aboard. He released the brake,
shook the reins, and they were off. The bouncing of the buckboard was as bone-jarring as the stage ride. Megan clenched
her teeth and held on. She wondered about her strange conversation with Susan Harrington.

Susan had been frightened at the mention of the Circle C.
Susan Harrington. Harrington. Hadn't that been the name she
had overheard Steve and Kip use that afternoon when they were
beside the stream?

"Steve?" Megan looked at his profile. "What is the problem
about the Circle C?"

He looked straight ahead, studying a moment before answering.

"I guess you'd better know." Looking at her, he held the reins
loosely and shifted slightly on the seat. "It seems we've bought
some trouble by coming out here. The Harringtons are the big
landholders, and they don't like squatters."

"But I thought you had deeded land."

"It is deeded. And that's exactly why I'm not backing down."
His jaw was set in a hard line. "Evidently, Harrington has some
pull around here, and he has some sort of claim on the Circle C.
The problem is that the law is in Denver. A deed is only a piece
of paper. Unfortunately, paper's not much protection against a
loaded six-shooter."

"You think there will be shooting?"

"No doubt there will." He glanced at Megan again. "Don't fret, though. I didn't fight under Bragg for nothing. We'll get through." He glanced at the sinking sun and clucked to the horses to get along faster.

The buckboard continued across the prairie to the rolling hills at the foot of the mountains. The horses started pulling and Steve slackened the reins to give them their head. Soon, prairie grasses were replaced by wildflowers, sagebrush, and piñon pine. A clean breeze swept over them as they neared the high country.

Megan gazed at the orange and brown rocks upthrust to the sky, the scrubby, green hillsides, and the jagged cliffs. She savored the scent of sage and pine. It was rugged country but she fell in love with it at first sight. Simply being there made her feel happier than she had in a long time.

"It's not far from here," Steve said when they passed over a rise. "I believe it's through this stretch of trees and across a stream.

"There it is!" Steve pulled the horses to a stop. A sprawling, thirty-acre meadow sloped gently up until it was cut off by a stone wall. On the eastern side of the wall were a stone cabin and a smaller gray building. The two buildings were joined by a high board fence. The setting sun shone full on them, bringing life to the rock wall and house. They glowed like bronze against the darkening sky.

It was more beautiful than Megan had imagined. A cooling gust of wind bathed her face. It felt refreshing after the long, hot days of traveling.

"Giddap!" Steve called to the team, and they rode slowly down the bank. The water came a few inches below the axle of the buckboard. Megan held her breath until they were climbing up the other side. Skirting the field, Steve held the horses to an even, moderate gate. Timothy grass brushed the bottom and sides of the buckboard.

By the time they reached the house the wind had taken on a definite chill. It pulled at Megan's dress and reached down inside of her. She picked up the shawl she had draped over the back of the seat and wrapped it closely around her shoulders. Shadows filled the hollows and crannies of the dooryard, bringing with them a strange foreboding. Uneasy, Megan looked around the dooryard that was little more than an extension of the meadow, full of thigh-high grass and brush. She pushed through the grass toward the stone house while Steve rummaged for a lantern and the lamp oil.

The floor and roof of the porch sagged wearily. A few boards were missing from each. The door leaned on cracked, dry leather hinges. The smell of dampness and mold caught at her nostrils. Resting her weight cautiously on the broken porch floor, she reached a tentative hand toward the door.

"Oh!" she cried sharply, drawing back. Inches from her face an enormous spider web covered the top half of the partly open door. Cringing, she pulled her shawl tightly about her and returned to the edge of the porch. The nightly cricket chorus had begun, punctuated now and then by the ghostly "who-o-o-o" of an owl.

She shivered, and dug her nails into the palms of her hands, holding in the discouraged, exhausted tears that sprang to her eyes. How could they sleep here tonight? And she yearned for a relaxing soak in a warm tub.

"Here's a lantern," Steve called from the buckboard fifteen minutes later. "I'd better see to a fire. It's getting cold." All she could see of him now was his middle, next to the swinging lantern held high above the tall grass as he walked toward her. Never giving the spider web a thought, he pushed the groaning door open and walked inside.

With many nervous glances, Megan squeezed herself into the smallest proportions possible and followed him into the gloomy house.

five

"There's a fire already laid," Steve said when he had set the lantern down. He knelt before the fireplace and struck a match on the edge of his boot sole. The dry wood sparked into a flickering flame.

Megan hovered nearby. She was afraid to move around or look too closely at the shadowy corners of the room. The fire gnawed with gathering appetite at the kindling, so Steve added a larger piece of wood. Megan felt a hint of warmth and moved even closer to the smoldering light.

"I'll bring in some things for the night." Steve stood up, brushing off his hands. "You sit down and rest yourself. You look all in."

"I'm sure a night's rest will set me right," she replied automatically as she moved to an upholstered settee near the fireplace and sank to the seat. Without another word, Steve took the lantern and stepped into the night.

In a few moments he was back carrying Megan's trunk with several blankets stacked on top. Working quickly and efficiently, he spread out a crude bed near the fire and told her to lie down. She felt her eyes drooping as soon as her head found a resting place.

❧

The cabin was dusky from sunlight shining through the cloudy windows when Megan awoke. Gingerly, she sat up. She ached in every bone, and her head throbbed dully. Steve was nowhere around.

A pail of water with a metal dipper hooked on the edge stood on the dusty stone hearth. Megan drank greedily, then bathed her face. She unlocked her trunk and was searching for a fresh dress when the door hinges groaned.

"Mornin'." Steve dropped an arm load of split logs into the wood box near the fireplace and brushed off his bark-flecked arms. "I'll move your things into the bedroom yonder if you want." He nodded toward a door on the wall opposite the front door. "I laid claim to the loft last night." He added a log to the small fire. "There's a spring out back if you want to wash up."

"I'll cook breakfast first," Megan responded. "I'm starving." She grinned in spite of herself.

Steve answered with a relieved smile. "The supplies we bought at Harper's are there." He pointed to two burlap sacks beside the moth-eaten settee. "I brought them in last night. You'd better use the fireplace until we can clean up the cookstove and check for a bird's nest in the chimney."

A hot breakfast improved Megan's outlook. She armed herself with soap and towel and went in search of the spring. Opening the back door, she peered outside. A wide stream of water flowed from a crack in the rock wall behind the house to fill a stone-lined basin in the ground. Through the clear water she could see the basin had some loose stones and moss inside, but it was in good condition. She touched the stream pouring down only to jerk her hand back. The water was like liquid ice.

The bath, though not quite the long soak of her daydream, was invigorating. While she finished dressing, she noticed that when the water left the basin it continued through a stone-paved trench that led through a springhouse and drained down a bank. Megan walked to the edge and looked down. Gasping, she took a step back. It was forty feet to the bottom! The eastern side of the house was on the edge of a small cliff.

Megan looked out at a vast expanse of blue-green rolling hills that melted to meet the level prairie. The sun was a glowing yellow ball barely resting on the flat horizon. The radiant light made the prairie grass gleam like silver as it swayed in the continuous breeze. She stood spellbound, feeling like an ant on the edge of an endless wilderness. No trace of human handi-work marred the landscape. It was magnificent.

How long she stayed there, she didn't know, but finally she realized she ought to get back to the business at hand and she turned away from the panorama with a promise to visit this spot many mornings in the future.

Back in the house, she wrapped a navy kerchief around her head, tied an old work apron over her blue calico dress, and made a careful, critical inspection of the house.

The front wall of the house was built of rock, and the floor was made of smooth, flat stones. Both walls and floor were fitted together as perfectly as a piece of pottery, broken and glued back together. The walls and open-beam ceiling were swaddled with dust-laden spider webs. The windows, cracked and pocked, were covered with a thick layer of fly-specked grime. There were two wooden chairs and a three-person settee positioned in a semicircle around the fireplace. The cushions were moldy and full of holes with small tufts of gray cotton showing through.

At the western end of the house was a dining area with the kitchen branching off toward the back, making an L shape. A thick oak table and four chairs were covered with the ever-present dust, but seemed in good condition.

Megan looked about her with an appraising eye. The marks of a craftsman were all around her. The house had definite possibilities.

She moved into the kitchen to examine the rusty range, two counters, and many cabinets. The single window revealed a small stretch of grass and one side of the gray wooden building she had seen last night. She also saw the high board fence.

The fence intrigued her. Why was it there? What did it hide? She went through the back door to find out the answer. When she had come out earlier, she was too taken up with the spring and the breathtaking view to think of looking in this direction.

The fence was six feet tall and parallel to the face of the rock wall, making a corridor about fifteen feet wide. Seeing nothing unusual behind the fence, Megan walked on until she came to the wooden building. Applying a little pressure, she lifted the reluctant door latch and was rewarded by a small shower of dirt when the door swung open.

She looked inside before she stepped over the doorsill. Six stalls stood before her with a single manger running the length of all six. The buckboard was beside the far wall, still loaded with the sacks of grain for the horses and the corn seed Steve had brought from Baltimore. On the wall near the open double doors hung a wooden bucket and a bit of chain. There was a door on the left side of the back wall, probably a ranch hand's modest quarters.

Steve stood in the second stall, a pitchfork in his hand.

"I was wondering where the fence led," she said when he looked up.

"This is a nice place, isn't it?" he asked without waiting for a reply. "I can say one thing for Cunningham, the man who built it." Steve rested his forearm on the pitchfork handle. "Besides being a craftsman, he knew how to prepare for a battle."

"A battle?"

"Sure. There's a rock wall behind the house, a cliff beside it, and no trees within shooting range. No one can approach the house unseen." He propped the pitchfork against the wall and picked up a shovel. "That fence was put there so he could get to his stock without going out in the open. And water back there, too."

"The house is well-made. I can see that."

"That's another thing. It has a stone front. The rest is made of squared logs. No bullet can get through them."

"You think he had a lot of trouble?"

Steve lifted a shovel full of hardened straw and manure from the floor and heaved it outside. "Judging from the town's reaction to us, I think it's pretty obvious," he answered, bending for another load.

"I guess I'd better get started in the house," she said in a moment and went back to the house the way she came.

It was noon when Megan walked out to the sagging front porch for a cold lunch and little rest. She was tired, but it was a satisfied feeling. The morning had been spent in the kitchen, for she couldn't tolerate the thought of no clean place in which to cook. She had scoured and scrubbed until her shoulders ached.

Steve joined her for bacon and biscuit sandwiches, leftovers from breakfast, and cold spring water. They passed the lunch break in companionable silence. In spite of the hard work, Megan was enjoying herself immensely. Those few minutes of sitting on the rickety porch, absorbing the blueness of the cloud-strewn sky and drinking in the hay-scented air, pumped life back into her tired limbs.

≈

It was past dark before Megan permitted herself another rest. The windows in the house were as clean as she could make them, cracked as they were, and the four-poster bed in her room had been stripped of its rotting mattress and replaced with a fresh hay-filled one. Steve had cut the hay from the front yard.

The kindred atmosphere of Steve sitting near the fire cleaning his new guns, thick stew bubbling cheerily on the shiny black kitchen stove, gave Megan a tender, contented feeling she hadn't known for a long, long time. She ladled the soup into bowls and set them carefully on the table.

"Tomorrow I'll scout around and get acquainted with the country," Steve said, drawing a knotted string through the barrel of his Winchester. "I left word at the livery stable, the hotel, and the Emporium that I need a hand. If we can't get one I'll have to work double to get the corn crop in. It'll be late as it is. Not to mention a garden."

Megan had to school herself to wash up after supper. She moved with leaden feet and arms but somehow she managed to finish. That night she lay alone in the darkness trying to sleep in spite of her sore shoulders and aching back. She pressed the heels of her hands against her eyes to ease her throbbing head.

It had been nine days since she had seen Jeremy. Was he better? Worse? How much longer would it be until she got some news? Her mind flitted from question to question. In a few minutes a soft rain started a soothing, tapping lullaby on her windowpane. The tune hushed her restless brain, and she fell asleep.

❧

The next morning Steve rode out before the sun shone its face full over the prairie. Megan stood in the doorway watching until horse and rider disappeared into the stand of oaks and pines. She was about to go inside when a movement in the tall grass caught her eye. She studied the edge of the yard, expecting to pick out a rabbit frozen in its tracks, when two pointed gray ears moved slightly at the edge of the grass.

She drew in a startled breath. *A wolf,* she thought. Even as the impression touched her consciousness, she rejected it. Wolves came at night and were shy of people.

The large gray head moved higher and came into her field of vision. The shaggy face ended in a pointed nose, further confirming her first impression, but there was a nagging doubt.

"Here, boy," she called softly. She spoke more to judge the animal's reaction than in hopes he would indeed come to her. The shaggy gray head bent down out of sight and raised up again. The mouth opened and its red tongue rolled out in a wide yawn, that ended in a low whine. The black button eyes were still fastened on her face.

It was a dog.

What is a dog doing so far from anyone? she wondered. She went inside for a leftover piece of biscuit from breakfast. She dredged the biscuit in partially hardened bacon drippings in the bottom of the frying pan. From the edge of the porch she threw the biscuit toward the dog as far as she could. It landed ten feet from him. Still watching her, he didn't move.

She waited a moment, decided she was wasting her time, and went back inside. She threw open all the windows in the house to let the clear, pine-scented air sweep through before clearing up the breakfast dishes.

That task finished, she glanced out at the spot where the biscuit had fallen. It was gone and so was the dog. Whether the dog or some other wild animal had taken the food, she couldn't tell. It was an unusual happening, but not significant and she forgot about it.

Late in the afternoon she was rubbing the wide, stone fireplace to a shine with pine oil when an odd sound stopped her in midmotion.

It was a voice as rough and rasping as a frog with laryngitis singing, "Rock of Ages, cleft for me, Let me hide myself in thee."

Half-curious and half-alarmed, Megan peered out a front window. Someone rode toward the house on a lop-eared, gray donkey.

"Let the water and the blood. . . ."

It was an old man wearing faded, dust-covered clothes and a brown Stetson with a frayed crown. He rode up to the porch and pulled up on the donkey's reins.

"Anybody to home?" he shouted.

With shaking fingers, Megan lifted the latch and stepped outside. The man swung from the saddle and took off his hat.

"Howdy, ma'am." He wasn't as old as Megan had first imagined. She was relieved to see his mild blue eyes had a friendly twinkle. "I heard you folks are needin' a hand."

"Yes," Megan said, smiling in response to his polite manner. "My husband is looking over the country today. I'm expecting him around supper time." She hesitated. "I've got some water on for coffee. Could I offer you a cup?"

"I'd be much obliged." He picked up the donkey's reins from where they trailed on the ground.

"You can put your donkey in the stable. There's a spring out back." Megan went back into the house to finish making the coffee.

"My name's Megan Chamberlin," she said as she handed him a steaming cup at the dining room table. "My husband is Steve."

"Thank you, ma'am. I'm Joe Calahan, but most folks call me Banjo on account of I'm always making music." He chuckled. "It seems like there's always a song on the inside o' me that's scramblin' to get out." He sipped his coffee, and sighed appreciatively. "That's a mighty fine cup, Mrs. Chamberlin. A good cup o' coffee is a great comfort to a man." With a work-gnarled hand he smoothed the spot on his graying black hair where his hat left a crease. "What type o' hand was your husband wantin'?"

"As far as I know, he's planning to put in a corn crop as soon as possible. He says it's almost too late already. He wants to get some cattle, too."

"I've turned my hand to just about ever'thin', so I reckon it don't much matter."

That evening when Megan introduced Banjo, Steve's relief was easy to see.

"After we mow the hay in the lower meadow, we can plant it in corn," Steve said after supper. They sat around the small flame in the fireplace. The June days were warm, but the nights still had a chill. The flickering firelight made the polished stones glow. "Know much about cattle?" he asked Banjo.

"I've punched a few cows," Banjo said. Thoughtfully, he rolled the toothpick he was chewing to the other side of his mouth. "Ever heard of the Harringtons?"

Megan started at the name.

"Kip Morgan told me a little about them."

"I know Kip. He's a good man. As for Victor Harrington, he was one of the first ranchers to open up this country. He fought off the Indians, built a ranch, and brought in about twenty thousand head o' cattle.

"He pushed out a few small ranchers in the process, but mostly folks stayed out o' his way. The bulk of the land he claims is government land, but the law is in Denver so government land or no don't make no difference. What he can hold with a six-shooter is his."

"That's what I figured," Steve said.

"I suppose you could try to do things through the law, but

that would only get Harrington to ride over to Denver and buy himself a lawyer, a judge, and a jury. You wouldn't have a Chinaman's chance.

"Well, sir." Banjo cleared his throat. "To get back to facts. Five or six years ago John Cunningham bought these four hundred acres. He came in quietlike and had this house pretty nigh built before Harrington got wind of it. You see, Harrington only comes around this neck o' the woods once in a blue moon. But there's plenty of water coming down off that mountain behind you. If there was to come a drought, he'd need that water in the worst way."

"I found a lake just south of here, too," added Steve.

"That's on your property," Banjo said, nodding. "Cunningham dug in for a long fight, and did a good job o' holding Harrington off, too. He had to go all the way to Denver for supplies there at the last, because Harrington put the strong arm on the shopkeepers in Juniper."

"Why did he quit?" Steve asked. "He'd done so much here."

"His wife died in childbirth. It took the heart out of him, I guess. I worked for him time and agin since he come here. A little over two years ago I was passin' through, and stopped by to swap howdies. He was gone." Banjo looked at Steve. "I never heard tell what became of him."

"I don't know much myself, Banjo," Steve answered. "He sold the property to my father about two years ago. I never saw him. My father left the land to me in his will. That's all I know."

"We'll be gettin' an early start, so I'd best say good night to you," Banjo said, rising. "Thank you for the fine meal, ma'am," he said, settling his hat on his head. "I'll be gettin' to my room in the stable." After Steve's return that afternoon they had swept out the back room of the stable and cut a new mattress full of hay for one of the two bunks. The quarters seemed bare to Megan but to Banjo, who had lived in many places like it or worse, it was homey.

"You're welcome, Banjo." Megan smiled. She was glad he had come.

six

The next morning when Megan glanced out the living room window, the same gray shaggy face she had seen the day before appeared at the edge of the meadow. The dog stayed still, ears high, watching the door of the house. Megan scooped a piece of bacon and the end of a loaf of bread from the table she had been clearing and darted for the porch. When she reached the door, she slowed down and was careful not to make any sudden moves. She stepped to the edge of the porch and threw the food toward him. The dog didn't flinch or make a move toward her.

"It's okay," she said, quietly. "I want to be your friend." After a few moments she decided the creature was not going to come closer and she went back inside. She made a mental note to tell the men when they came back that afternoon. The stray dog intrigued her. She wished she could learn more about where he came from.

಴

The sun was slipping down behind the mountains the next day when a group of riders appeared at the edge of the meadow and galloped toward the house. Hearing the hoofbeats, Megan came to the open doorway to watch. Steve and Banjo were on their way to the house for supper when the group reached the dooryard.

"You Chamberlin?" A wafer-thin, freckled young man with a thick crop of fiery red hair stepped his pinto horse to the front.

"I'm Chamberlin," Steve acknowledged.

"You get out," the red-haired young man ordered in a strident voice. His hard, green eyes looked down coldly at Steve.

"This here's Rocking H range, and we don't cotton to squatters."

"I've got a deed for this land," replied Steve, his voice still even, "and I don't bluff." He looked around the group of five riders. "You fellows are welcome if you come peaceable. Otherwise, consider yourselves warned."

The leader edged his horse forward until it almost touched Steve. "You consider yourself warned." He dropped his hand toward his holster.

"Easy, Beau."

Beau hesitated and looked toward a tall, black-haired man with a narrow face and a deep scar running from his temple to his jaw. The man who spoke stepped his horse forward three steps. He was chewing thoughtfully on a twig.

"They'll git what's comin' to 'em if they don't go. No need to fly off the handle. Your pa don't want shootin' trouble. We can handle 'em another way."

"You heard my answer." Steve stood straight, right hand tense and ready beside his six-shooter. "Now, get off my land."

Four of the riders turned their horses, but the one with the red hair hesitated. He looked scornfully at Banjo.

"You joinin' this outfit, Banjo?"

"That's right, Harrington." Banjo's twinkle was nowhere to be seen. "I'm with 'em. And you'll get a run for your money."

Beau considered this news, then slowly turned his horse. "Get out!" he repeated and joined his friends.

Megan was shaky with relief and alarm when the group of men rode off. She went inside to set the table, but her ears were tuned to hear Banjo's comments on the incident.

"That Harrington's son?" Steve asked Banjo when he came in from washing up in the basin out back.

"In the flesh," Banjo said, pulling out a chair and sitting to the table. "He's like a banty rooster. His pa's the big rooster, and he tries to carry the same weight." He glanced at Steve.

"But don't underestimate him. He's mean as a snake. I was in town one time when a stranger called him 'Red.' He bumped into Beau and said, 'Sorry, Red,' just like that. Well, sir, the young feller hauled iron and that hombre almost got hisself shot. If Clyde Turner, the feller with the scar, hadn't been there, who knows what would have happened. That boy's mighty techy about his hair."

"Who's Turner?" Steve asked, forking a piece of beef on his plate.

"He's the foreman. Been with Harrington five, six years."

"He looks familiar, but I can't place him."

"He scares me," Megan said, shivering. "Both of them do."

"Don't alarm yourself, Miss Megan," Banjo said, setting down his coffee cup and smiling kindly. "There's not many men in these parts would harm a lady."

Banjo's words were small comfort when Megan thought of all that was at stake for her in this lonesome place. What if Steve were killed, or they had to leave? What would happen to Jeremy? She brooded over those questions until she was worn out with thinking. They had to make it.

❧

Fear tightened Megan's lips and creased her brow as she watched Steve strap on his gunbelt before leaving the house the next morning. He noticed her anxious expression and paused at the door.

"A gun is a tool out here, Megan. I'm not asking for trouble by wearing it, just preparing in case it comes."

"I know," she said, tearing her gaze from the gun to meet his eyes. "But it frightens me to think of what could happen. Please be careful." Through the window she watched him cross the distance to the stable. By sheer will she forced down the fear and went about her chores.

❧

Three days after Harrington's visit Steve pulled his shiny new plow from the stable and hitched up Star before dawn. They had a long day in store for them planting their garden, and Megan would work alongside the men. The black was restless, eager to get going. He bobbed his head and blew until Steve took the reins, and they walked across the freshly cut meadow. Banjo followed him carrying a hoe over his shoulder and his old buffalo gun in the crook of his arm.

Megan finished the breakfast dishes and packed a lunch before she followed the men to the large, sunny plot near the stream at the western edge of the meadow. She carried a cloth-covered basket on her arm and many small sacks of seeds in her apron pocket. The air was sweet with the smell of newly cut timothy. A playful breeze made the wide brim of her sunbonnet flap up and down. It tugged at her full skirt, wrapping the cloth around her ankles so she almost tripped. She heard birds twittering in the woods. The beauty of the morning made her want to spread her arms wide and twirl around until she had to sit down for dizziness.

"There's power in the blood, power in the blood." Banjo's hearty voice drifted with the breeze.

What does he have to sing about? He seems so poor and alone. Like me. But he's used to it, she decided. He's probably always lived like that.

"Beautiful day, Miss Megan," Banjo called, cheerfully. He knocked his hat to the back of his head and wiped his brow on his sleeve. "That sun'll be mighty hot come noon, though."

Onions, carrots, green beans, and limas—she set the sacks of seeds near a cottonwood tree. She'd already put tomato, cabbage, and sweet potato seeds to sprout in a tray in the kitchen. Peas, turnips. . .she could almost taste them already.

"What should I do first?" Megan asked Steve, waiting on the edge of the plowed plot.

"Banjo will hoe you a furrow. You follow along and drop the seeds in. He'll tell you how." Calling to the horse, Steve bent over the plow handles and moved slowly away, cutting a brown strip from the edge of the meadow.

"Banjo, I've been meaning to ask you something, but I keep forgetting about it." Megan was dropping green bean seeds into a furrow three steps behind Banjo. The sun was high in the cloudless sky.

"What's that?" He didn't look up. His hoe kept chopping and pulling back the dark earth.

"A strange dog comes to the edge of the meadow every morning. When the grass was tall, he'd stay hidden, but since the meadow has been cut he sort of crawls up to the edge of the yard on his belly and crouches there. At first I thought he was a wolf, but he's got some brown and black patches on his back, and he whines sometimes when he sees me. I was wondering if he may have belonged to Cunningham."

Banjo paused to mop his brow with a splotchy handkerchief. "Now that you mention it, I believe Cunningham did have a dog. I never paid much mind." He stuffed the handkerchief into his back pocket and bent over the hoe. "If I saw the critter, I could tell you if it's the same one."

"I've been throwing food out to him but he hasn't come to get it while I'm outside. I've watched from the window. He never barks or growls, just whines."

"I'll have to get a look at him."

"Maybe Steve will be ready to break for lunch soon." She put her hands on the small of her back and leaned backward. "It will be noon shortly. I'll ask him the next time he comes close to this end of the garden."

An hour later, the men sprawled on the ground under an oak tree, and Megan spread out a blue-checkered cloth to serve sandwiches. She tried not to notice her dirt-stained hands and rough nails. They were still ugly, though she had scrubbed vigorously in the stream.

"You in Mr. Lincoln's War?" Banjo asked Steve. The sun

now was glaring down upon the garden plot, and the shade of the trees was a welcome relief.

"Fortieth Mississippi." Steve lounged against a tree, chewing a long piece of grass.

"I served under Sheridan the last few years of the war," Banjo continued. "I lived in Texas then, you know." He leaned back until he was resting on one elbow. After some talk and laughter they rose and went back to work.

It was close to dusk when Megan plodded wearily back to the house. She turned to look back at Steve and Banjo finishing the last strip of rich, brown earth. Tired as she was, it was gratifying to know she belonged here. This was her own home and these were her men to care for, at least for now. If only Jeremy were here, and Em. She tried to push aside the anguish that lingered in the back of her mind ready to steal every morsel of happiness she might know here.

※

During the next several weeks life on the ranch fell into a routine. Day by day Megan worked in the garden pulling out the weeds until her hands became tough and strong. Her face grew tan in spite of the sunbonnet she wore. It wasn't long before she grew to love the smell and feel of rich earth.

The morning Steve came to tell her his news, she was on hands and knees seeking out the latest interlopers among the two-inch-high sprouts. She stood and brushed the dirt from her hands when he came near.

"Banjo and I will be leaving for a few days," he said. "He tells me Jim Sanders, the owner of the Running M, may sell me some cattle. I want to get several hundred head to fatten up before winter."

"How long will you be gone?" Megan tried to hide her dismay. How would she feel being at home alone?

"It'll only be two or three days. I'd like to leave tomorrow if I can finish putting in the corn today."

Megan looked at the lower meadow, all plowed and planted except for a small patch. Steve had chosen the lower ten acres so the edge of the field would still be out of shooting range when the corn grew tall. She swallowed to ease the tightness in her throat.

"All right. I'll bake some biscuits for you to take along."

"You've done well for a city girl, Megan." He smiled down at her. Megan looked away, her cheeks burning.

His smile stayed with her when he and Banjo rode out the next morning. It warmed her inside where she couldn't reach. When the men disappeared from her sight she lingered at the open door watching for a familiar face at the edge of the yard. As usual, a shaggy gray figure came to rest just beyond her throwing range.

"Here, boy," she called again. She held out a piece of bacon rind. "Come on. I won't hurt you."

The dog moved forward a pace and sat down. He tilted his head to one side and whined.

"What are you afraid of?" she kept talking in a soothing voice. With an underhanded throw, she tossed the meat. It landed near his feet. "I won't hurt you, you know. I would like to be friends." She continued cajoling and coaxing a few moments longer. The dishes were waiting, as always, and finally she decided to go back inside and attend to them.

Before she moved, the dog crouched down and crawled to the bit of bacon. Grasping it in his teeth, he backed to the edge of the grass to eat it, always watching Megan.

"Well, you're getting braver, are you?" She went inside for a piece of bread and threw it to him. "Friends. See?" She brushed a crumb from her hand. "You could use a friend. . .and so could I." With a last wistful smile, she went inside the house.

❧

That day Megan cleaned the loft, taking advantage of Steve's absence, and made doughnuts for his return. The dog returned the next morning. Megan sat on the steps and talked to him for half an hour. He watched her closely and whined twice, but he wouldn't come near.

Early in the afternoon of the second day she was spreading out some navy gingham to make a tablecloth when movement at the edge of the meadow caught her eye. She ran to the window for a closer look. The sight filled her with horror.

Several men on horses circled the garden. One had flaming red hair and rode a piebald pinto.

Beau Harrington.

With a motion inviting the others to follow, he stepped his horse into the garden and began tramping around.

At first Megan couldn't move. She stood, mouth open, staring as they started through the garden plot. Abruptly, she came to herself. Indignation grew into outrage and she overcame her natural fear. She ran to the fireplace, tore Steve's extra rifle from its pegs above the mantel shelf, and raced outside, holding it clumsily in her arms.

"Stop! Stop!" she shouted. One time she almost stumbled on the rough ground, but she never stopped or even hesitated. She ran to the edge of the garden and awkwardly raised the rifle. "Stop, or I'll shoot!"

"Well, well," Beau Harrington was the first to speak, "what have we here? Chamberlin lettin' a woman do his fightin' for him now?"

"He's not here or he'd take on the lot of you," Megan fumed. She raised the gun higher. "But it doesn't take a man's finger to pull a trigger. You get out of here before I do."

"She means it, boss." A long-legged, skinny man with a beak nose spoke up. He watched Megan warily.

"Slim's right," Clyde Turner added. His flinty eyes sized up Megan and the long gun in her arms.

"You tell your man he can expect more of the same if he doesn't move," Beau sneered. He hesitated after the others moved away, then slowly followed them.

The closer Megan came to the house the weaker her knees became, the sicker her stomach felt. Her arms were too limp to lift the rifle back to its pegs so she propped it against the wall and sank into a chair. She realized tears were streaming down her face. Covering her face with her hands, she gave way to frustrated sobs.

Their beautiful crop was ruined. Crying relieved some of her pent-up emotions, and she stared blindly at the cold fireplace. After the first waves of despair had passed, discouragement slowly transformed into smoldering anger.

How dare those scoundrels! She wouldn't let the likes of Beau Harrington stop her. Too much was at stake.

She washed her face in the spring. Weren't there some seeds left? Yes, the sacks were in the kitchen. Armed with a hoe and the Henry, she marched out to inspect the damage. She glanced at the sun, still high above the horizon. If she hurried there may be time to make repairs before dark.

Kneeling over her injured seedlings, she discovered the damage wasn't as overwhelming as she first thought. She crept along on all fours, straightening a seedling here, planting new seeds there until the sun sank low and the seeds were spent. She stood and stretched her tired back as she looked over her work. It wasn't as large as it had once been, but there would still be fresh vegetables on their table.

Candy came to the fence and nickered when Megan walked past the corral. She propped the hoe and rifle against a post and rubbed the roan's nose. *I wonder if I can still ride,* she thought, resting her aching forehead against the mare's smooth cheek. *One of these days,* she promised herself, *I'll give it a try.*

❧

It was noon the next day when Kelsey, Banjo's lop-eared donkey, stepped out of the trees. Billy wasn't far behind. Was that a third horse with them? Megan strained her eyes but couldn't tell. Quickly, she slid her freshly risen rolls into the oven, smoothed her hair, and ran out to meet them.

"There is a fountain filled with blood, drawn from Emmanuel's veins. . . ." It was Banjo's voice, as sweet and rough as ever. "And sinner's plunged beneath its flood lose all their guilty stains. Hello, Miss Megan." Banjo smiled warmly and raised his hat.

"We brought you something." Steve stepped out of the saddle on the off side and came around his horse holding a rope. Slowly, a short black and white animal followed.

"A cow!" Megan clapped her hands in delight.

"Sanders had two, and this one just weaned a heifer calf so he let me have her. For a price, you understand." He chuckled wryly. "She's a Holstein. They're supposed to be good milkers. Her name's Bess."

"She's beautiful!" Megan couldn't take her eyes off the creature. "Oh, Steve! A cow! We haven't had milk, or butter, or cheese for ages."

"We bought eight hundred head of longhorns from Sanders, too. We left them in a grassy canyon east of here. A nice looking lot, don't you think, Banjo?"

"Nice as I've ever seen." Banjo's eyes twinkled at Megan's enraptured exclamations over Bess.

"Oh, I've rolls in the oven." Megan lifted her wide skirt to free her ankles and ran lightly to the house. Banjo's chuckle followed her.

"We had some visitors while you were gone." Megan brought up the awful affair after the men had enjoyed a hot meal. They were relaxing over a second cup of coffee. "Beau Harrington and his hands."

"What did they do?" Steve sat up straight and stared at her, an unpleasant light in his eyes.

"They trampled the garden." She was worried by the thundercloud forming on Steve's face. "It wasn't as bad as I first imagined. I guess I stopped them in time."

"You what?"

"I took the rifle from over the fireplace and ran out and stopped them. I told them I'd shoot if they didn't go."

"They give you any trouble?" Steve's face matched the glowing embers in the smoldering fireplace.

"The red-haired one had his usual bluster, but the rest were ready to leave soon enough, I reckon."

"I guess they had good reason," Banjo said, dryly. "Facin' a man with a gun is one thing. Facin' a wrought-up woman with one is another'n."

Steve scraped his chair back and stood to his feet. "I'm going over there and have it out with Harrington."

His words were like a heavy millstone crushing the breath from Megan's lungs. "You'll be on their land," she protested. "There's no telling what may happen."

"This foolishness has got to stop, Megan," he insisted, clapping on his hat. "Harrington needs to learn a lesson. I reckon I'm the one elected to teach him." He flipped his gunbelt around his waist and buckled it with a quick, practiced motion.

"Please, Steve," she pleaded, following him to the door. "They'll kill you if they get a chance."

"I'm going to put a stop to this kind of thing once and for all."

She reached for his arm, but he brushed her away and strode to the stable. In a few moments he galloped away on Caesar. Megan pressed her fist to her mouth to quench a silent sob as he disappeared into the trees.

seven

Banjo joined Megan in the doorway as Caesar's hoofbeats faded into the distance. "He's got to do it you know."

"I know." Megan was still fighting tears. She was so afraid. "Are we going to win, Banjo? Do we have any chance of holding onto the Circle C against the Harringtons?"

Banjo didn't answer for a long minute. He stared across the meadow toward the setting sun. "Miss Megan," he finally answered, "I'm not a prophet like Elijah so I can't tell the future for sure, but I will tell you this. The three of us are gonna make a brass-plated effort. That's all we can do. We'll have to leave it in the hands of the good Lord after we've done our best."

Without speaking any more the old cowhand and the young wife lingered in the last light of day. Neither of them wanted to go back into the shadowy house.

"Did you have the safety off?" Banjo asked when the sky was indigo with a dull yellow glow rimming the mountains.

"The what?"

"The safety on the Henry. If you don't take the safety off, it won't shoot."

"I just picked it up and ran out, so I reckon I didn't."

"Ho, Ho!" Banjo guffawed. "You chased those rascals away with the safety still on." He enjoyed a good chuckle then became serious. "You ought to learn to shoot. Most women out here do."

"Would you teach me, Banjo?"

"Well," he drawled, slowly, "you'd best ask your husband first. If he doesn't have time, I'll be happy to."

Megan flushed, realizing her slip. Confused, she chose that

61

moment to clear away the supper dishes, hoping he hadn't noticed.

ঌ

Megan was pacing the floor when Steve rode in late that night. Banjo had gone to his room in the stable. Steve's step was slow and heavy on the creaky porch.

"What happened?" she asked anxiously as soon as he stepped into the light.

"No one was there. Only one I could round up was the cook, and he said everybody was in town. By the time I got there I'd cooled off some. There was no good could come of going off half-cocked." He hung his hat and gunbelt on their pegs and flung himself on the settee. "So, I came on home."

"I kept some coffee hot for you."

"That would taste mighty good." He rubbed the back of his neck and stretched out his legs. "I guess we'll have to hold on and see what happens. Banjo's right, you know. With the law all the way in Denver, we'll have to fight it out ourselves." He took the steaming mug from Megan. "Thanks. That's exactly what I needed after a day like today."

"Will you teach me to shoot?" She sat in the chair near the fireplace.

"Teach you to shoot?" He looked up. "Sure. I was figuring on putting in some practice time myself." He sipped his coffee. "You've got to get the troops in order before you can go to war."

ঌ

Megan tried to write a cheery letter to Jeremy the next day, but the words wouldn't come. She had been in Colorado for more than a month and still had had no word from Em. After several false starts she managed a bright description of the ranch and the garden. She described the four horses and Banjo's donkey in detail, knowing he would like to hear about them. With a heavy heart, she sealed the envelope.

Surely Jeremy wasn't worse. Could that be why Em hadn't asked someone to pen down a note for her? Tormented by doubts and fears, a dark cloud settled over Megan's spirit. Not knowing what was happening back in Baltimore was harder to bear than being there and facing the worst.

The days that followed were long and tedious. She spoke little and smiled less. Every rider that came into the meadow struck new fear in Megan's heart.

The afternoon a big palomino stepped into view she was churning butter on the porch, hoping to catch a passing breeze. Instead of riding to the house, the tall stranger rode to the corral where Banjo was stringing barbed wire around a fence post. Megan was relieved to see Banjo raise his hand in greeting and straighten to talk. The rider stayed only minutes and rode away.

Brimming with questions, she took a cup of water out to Banjo later to give herself an excuse to talk to him.

"Who rode in this afternoon, Banjo? Did you know him?"

"That was Wyatt Hammond, Harrington's horse wrangler." He smiled at Megan's alarm. "Don't fret yourself. He's a fine young man. I knowed his folks. He's a different brand than that red-topped sapling. Wyatt was on his way to town and stopped to swap howdies.

"Somethin' troublin' you I could help with, Miss Megan?" He gave her a questioning, fatherly smile, his frayed felt hat knocked to the back of his head.

"It's nothing really, Banjo." She tried to smile back at him but only half succeeded. "I haven't had any word from my little brother, that's all. He's in a sanitarium in Baltimore with rheumatic fever. I guess I've been letting my worries show too much."

"That's what friends are for, you know, helping carry burdens." He hesitated a moment before adding, "I have a Friend Who carries all my burdens."

Megan looked at him, waiting for him to continue.

"His name is Jesus. He's been carrying my burdens for almost fifteen years now."

"You don't have many burdens, Banjo. You are always so happy."

"You know what I said about being from Texas? My wife and I had a ranch a few miles south of the Red River. Purtiest little place you ever did see. We worked the land and ran some cows, kind o' like you and Steve. It was a good life. We had a son, a lively little lad. He used to foller me around like a little shadow." He cleared his throat.

"It was back in '58. I had to go away for a few days to take care of some business. While I was gone Kiowas burned the ranch. They killed Mary and took my son." His eyes filled with tears. He swallowed and went on. "Mary was a good Christian but I wasn't, then. I wandered around for a while, not sure what to do or where to go. After a few years I joined Sheridan. I figured I didn't have much more to lose.

"A young preacher came out to the troops and held some meetin's. He preached right to me. I knew Mary was in heaven, and I wasn't goin' there. After one of the meetin's, I went up and talked with that preacher. He showed me how to make my peace with God. Jesus has been my best Friend ever since." He smiled gently. "I know He'd help you, too, if you asked Him."

His words came back to her later that evening. How could he be so happy not knowing if his son was alive or dead? *He must be a strong person,* Megan decided. *I don't have that kind of courage.*

☙

Steve spent most evenings behind the corral practicing with his six-shooter. At first Megan jumped every time he fired a shot, but eventually she became accustomed to the noise. One day she ventured out to see if he would teach her how to handle a gun.

Surprise made her hesitate when she saw him. Instead of a pistol he held a double-edged knife, poised to throw. He rose up on the balls of his feet, paused a second, and threw the knife into a straw target he had set up, a perfect hit. He walked over to pull the knife out, and stopped short when he saw her.

"So, you've discovered my secret weapon," he said, walking

toward her. "When I was in the army, we'd practice throwing to pass the time. I was pretty good at it then. I'm a little rusty now."

"I'd like to learn to shoot."

"Oh, yes. I remember you mentioning it." He looked at his guns lying on a flat rock nearby. "Which would you prefer, the pistol or the rifle?"

"I don't know."

He picked up the pistol and handed it to her. "Try this and see how it feels."

"It's awful heavy," she said, holding it with two hands.

"See if you can raise it at arm's length."

Her arm wobbled as she struggled to keep the barrel up. "Let's try the Henry." He took the pistol from her. "You can use both hands to hold it and balance it on your shoulder." The rifle was awkward. She couldn't tell where to put her hands on it. Steve adjusted her grip. "Lift it shoulder high and sight along the barrel. Aim at that tree trunk." He pointed to a pine thirty feet away. "Start at the base of the tree and follow it up."

Megan grasped the gun tightly, one hand on the trigger, one on the barrel. Taking a breath to calm herself, she lifted the rifle.

"Gently work the trigger. You feel the slack there?"

"Yes." She moistened her lips.

"Slowly take in the slack, and squeeze off a shot real gentle-like. Try for that slash in the bark about eye level. You see it?"

"I see it." Biting her bottom lip, she concentrated on that mark and squeezed gently, like he said.

BOOM!

The slam of the rifle against her shoulder made her step back. Her heel sank into a small hole, throwing her off balance. She sat down hard. Her shoulder was burning dreadfully. It must be black and blue.

"You hit it! You hit it!" He walked over to examine the tree. "A little to the left and a tad high, but you hit it."

"I think it hit me." She rubbed her sore shoulder.

He was beside her in four strides. "Are you hurt?" He knelt down beside her, concern in his eyes.

"My shoulder's bruised, but besides that it's only my pride, I guess." She looked at him accusingly. "Why didn't you warn me?"

"About the kick? I guess I forgot. I'm sure sorry." He helped her up. "Don't rest the butt on your shoulder from now on. Hold it a little away if you can, or let it rest on top of you shoulder." He brushed dirt from her arm. "Do you want to quit for today?"

"I came to learn and learn I aim to do." She straightened her skirt and picked up the rifle. "What were you saying about more to the left?"

With that, target practice became a daily ritual and, before many days passed, she could hit a leaf at fifty yards.

"You're a natural shot, Megan," Steve said after practice two weeks later. "You've got a steady hand and a keen eye. Just remember the Henry shoots a little high and to the left."

Megan thrived on these times of easy companionship with Steve. He was a patient teacher, and she liked to hear him talk. It gave her a contented, restful feeling to be with him and share things with him.

❧

"I'm going to ride into town tomorrow," Steve said one evening in mid-July on their walk back to the house. "Is there anything you need?"

"You can mail a letter for me and check the post office," she replied, quickly. "Besides that, there are a few groceries. A little sugar, molasses, things like that."

"Banjo will be around if you need him. I want to get some nails to repair the porch and some glass for the windows."

But the next morning, when Steve drove the buckboard around the meadow, a strange emptiness swept over Megan. It was odd she should feel that way since Banjo was still nearby.

She tried to brush it away but it kept creeping back.

Her spirits lifted later when her doggy friend crept to the porch to get a pancake lying on the ground near the steps. Megan had thrown it there to tempt him.

"Banjo," she called in the same voice she used when talking to the dog. "Banjo, come here."

Banjo appeared in the stable doorway. Megan placed a warning finger on her lips and pointed to the dog hungrily chewing the pancake. She threw down another when the animal looked up at her.

It was the first time she'd had a complete look at him. He was shaggy from his bearded cheeks to his feathery tail, a big dog, but not as large as some. His hips made bony points at his back end. He had black, brown, and white patches on his back and sides. The rest of him was the color of dirty mop water.

"Would you like a third?" she asked, holding up her last offering. The dog sat down, eyes boring into the pancake. "Here you go." She threw it to him. "I always was an easy mark for a hungry stomach."

The dog seemed to sense there was no more food to be had. He picked up the pancake and trotted away.

"That's Cunningham's dog, all right," Banjo said, walking toward her. "Used to follow him everywheres."

"What's his name?" Megan excitedly voiced the question she'd wondered every morning these past six weeks.

"I don't know." The wrinkles in his brow deepened while he searched his memory. "I can't remember Cunningham calling him. I'm sure he must have, but it didn't stick with me." He grinned at her disappointed face. "Sorry, Miss Megan. Why don't you name him yourself? He'll pick up a new name soon enough, I reckon." He took off his hat to scratch the back of his head. "Do you mind me asking why you're so interested in a stray dog?"

"I can't really say, Banjo. I guess it's because he seems so alone. And he's starving. I guess I feel sorry for him."

"Keep workin' on him. He'll get used to you in time." He

adjusted his hat and clumped back to the stable. Megan took a last look at the grass where the dog disappeared. What could she name him?

⋙

Megan was knotting a rag rug to put in front of the hearth and thinking about dog names when she heard galloping hoofbeats. Dropping her work she looked nervously out the window.

A large, chestnut horse came at full tilt around the green field of knee-high corn waving gently in the breeze. A wiry man in a red plaid shirt and Levi's leaned over the saddle. Horse and rider slowed to a trot at the edge of the yard and came to a halt in front of the porch. The man swung down in an easy, lithe movement. Megan blinked her eyes and looked again.

Instead of a man, it was a tall, slim young woman wearing men's clothes, the same girl she had met in Harper's Emporium the day they arrived in Juniper Junction. Relieved and glad, Megan opened the door.

"Hello." The young woman took off her light brown Stetson, revealing her thick blond mane, full of strawberry highlights in the sun. "I'm Susan Harrington, remember?"

"Yes, of course." Megan smiled broadly. "Please come in." She was delighted to have feminine companionship. "Would you like some tea? I'll put the kettle on."

"How lovely!" Susan exclaimed when she entered the house. "I've always liked stone better than logs. And blue calico!" She gave the living room curtains a loving touch.

It was true the house had undergone a transformation under Megan's skillful hand. The floors shone with a coating of linseed oil. A blue-checked tablecloth and matching curtains made the dining room a cheery nook. The kitchen range gleamed with a fresh coating of stove blacking, all signs of rust banished. A white gauze curtain dressed the kitchen window, and the linoleum, though worn, was well-scrubbed.

"Please sit down," Megan said when she returned from the kitchen.

Susan perched on the edge of a chair, holding her hat in her hands.

"I came because. . . ," Susan avoided Megan's eyes, "because I heard about what happened to your garden. I wanted you to know how sorry I am." She glanced at Megan. "I overheard some of the men talking when I was in the stable getting ready to ride this morning." She paused and drew in a deep breath. "It was Beau's doing. I know it."

"I hope the land dispute won't affect our friendship," Megan said sincerely. "I've thought about you several times since we met in Juniper. I was hoping we could get acquainted."

Susan's troubled face brightened. She watched Megan's smooth movements while pouring tea into two cups.

"Beau's always trying to prove something," she went on impulsively. "He scares me. If it wasn't for Wyatt—" She broke off and quickly sipped her tea.

"We didn't come here to cause trouble," Megan said, resuming her seat. "My husband has a deed to this land. It's his, and he wants to keep it, that's all."

"I wish Pa wasn't so set on having this place," Susan said, wistfully. "You aren't the only ones he's been against, believe me. A year ago he accused Jim Sanders of rustling. Elaine Sanders is one of my friends. I tried to tell Pa Jim wouldn't do such a thing, but he wouldn't listen." She sighed. "Since Ma died, he won't listen to anyone." A brittle edge crept into her voice. "All he thinks about are his precious cattle." She shook her head, and smiled at Megan. "Do you ride?"

"I used to when I was a child. I haven't tried lately."

"You should. We could go riding together."

"Do you always go off alone?" Megan asked, wonderingly.

"Sure. No one will bother me. Unless I surprise some Indians or something." She laughed at Megan's alarmed expression. "We haven't had Indian trouble for a year or so. Mostly they stay on the prairie these days. Anyway, I can shoot."

"I'd like to go riding," Megan admitted. "I'll practice a little, and maybe we can go." She looked at Susan's rugged costume. "I'll have to find something to wear."

"These are my brother's clothes. Most western women don't wear citified riding clothes, but you can if you want."

"I have an old riding costume that used to be my mother's. I do want to come."

"That would be nice." Susan set down her teacup and rose. "I'd best be going. I'll come around after a while and see if you are ready to ride with me."

"All right." Megan walked to the door with the slim woman. "I'm so glad you came. I was feeling a bit lonely today."

"And thanks for understanding about Beau." Susan turned impulsively and put her hand on Megan's arm. "I wish there was more I could do."

Before Megan could answer, Susan put on her hat, stepped across the sagging porch, and was gone. Megan gazed long at the cloudless blue sky, meditating on the visit. Poor Susan, living with a negligent father and a hot-tempered brother. At that moment Megan determined that no matter what the future held, she would try to be Susan's friend.

క

The hour drew late, and Steve did not come. Banjo sat with Megan in the light of two coal oil lamps while she read *The Pilgrim's Progress* aloud to pass the time. She forced herself not to look out the window, trusting her ears to tell her of Steve's arrival. Her nerves were frayed to a ragged edge when the hoofbeats she had been yearning to hear resounded in the dooryard.

"He's back." She dropped the book on the table and ran to the door.

"I'll take the hull off his horse." Banjo grabbed his hat from a peg near the door and was gone.

Megan stood on the porch, straining to see through the darkness. A wide, yellow crescent of light from the open door fell over Steve's face as he stepped up. The sight made her gasp.

eight

Both of Steve's eyes were black and blue, one almost swelled shut, and there was a wide, ugly gash over his left cheekbone. His lower lip was cut and puffy. He held his right arm close to his side, and that battered hand was twice its normal size. He made a rasping sound when he breathed. Like a sleepwalker, he shuffled over to the settee and sank to the seat as though the presence of the sofa was all that kept him from collapsing altogether. Several seconds passed before he could speak.

"Four or five of Harrington's men jumped me outside of Harper's." His voice was thick with pain. He grunted a little with each breath. "One of them clubbed me on the head from behind and knocked me down for the others to pound me. I couldn't see who they were, it happened so fast, but I heard that red-haired villain's voice." He stopped to take two ragged breaths. "I guess I passed out. When I came around it was almost dark. I wasn't in any shape to go looking for them, so I got the hostler to hitch the team for me and came home."

"You should have seen a doctor before you came out here." Megan stood near him, staring, shocked at the brutality of his injuries. She didn't like the sound of his breathing at all.

"Knew you'd be worried," he continued. "The doc might have wanted me to hang around and I didn't want to." He grimaced in pain and held his side. "You got a letter." Fumbling, he pulled a wrinkled envelope from his shirt pocket and handed it to her.

Megan's heart lurched as she took the letter. She smoothed it lovingly between her hands before she lay it on the table and rushed to the kitchen for hot water and a towel. Gently, she bathed Steve's face and hand, cringing at what she found under the dirt and dried blood.

"I don't think there are any broken bones," she decided as he slowly moved his fingers. "At least not in your hand." She was thinking of his ribs and the sound of his labored breathing.

"The hand won't be any good to me for a while, though." He stared at the purple, swollen flesh. "Right now I'd like to be able to use an iron mighty bad."

"That cut on your cheek has to be closed," Megan went on, ignoring his remark. "It's lying wide open. I've got some tape in the kitchen.

"Mama and I patched up many a soldier when we were in Virginia," she chattered to ease the mood when she returned with tape and bandages. "There was a lot of fighting around Fredricksburg, you know." Her hands moved steadily, efficiently, as she talked. "We changed bandages, served meals, and did anything else that was needed in the hospital after our plantation burned. I guess we bandaged as many Yanks as we did Confederates." She pressed the last piece of tape on his cheek.

"Now, let's take a look at those ribs."

"My ribs are all right," Steve protested, straightening.

"Yes, that's why you've been breathing so easily." Immovable as the rock wall behind the house, she met his eyes. "Let's have a look."

Never taking his eyes from her face, he slowly reached for his shirt buttons. In short order his ribs were bound tightly with a long, three-inch-wide strip of cloth. It was near midnight when he paused at the foot of the ladder to the loft. He put his foot on the first run and paused, looking at her.

"Thanks."

"Get some rest," she replied lightly.

Bone tired though she was, she brought the treasured envelope close to the coal oil lamp and tore it open with shaking fingers. The words ran together when she tried to read. She squeezed her eyes shut, willing them to focus, and tried again.

Dear Miss Megan,

    Just wanted you to know we got your tellygram. Jeremy is doing good. Always talks about them horses you got. He can't git out of bed yet, tho. Doc says he'll be abed about two more months. Don't fret none. This was writ by my landlady, Mrs. Osgood.

Sincerely,
Em

After reading the note three times to wring every ounce of home from it that she could, she put the letter carefully in her trunk. She lay wide-eyed in the darkness thinking of Jeremy and Em, and the home they used to share. She ached to put her arms around him once more, to see him smile, to hear him laugh. The lump in her throat choked her. She turned her face into her pillow and sobbed.

ã*

The next morning Banjo came to the house carrying a small pasteboard box. He tapped on the door and beamed at Megan when she opened it.

"Since when do you have to knock?" Megan peered curiously at the box. "What's that?"

"Look for yourself." He held out the box for her to take a look. "Chickens."

Megan was too tired and emotionally spent to be excited at Banjo's announcement.

"Steve brought them. He brought a passel of other things, too. The wagon was loaded down." He glanced at Megan's serious face. "How is he?"

"Two cracked ribs, one of them may be broken. A horribly bruised hand, and a beat-up face. I think he'll be all right, though, as long as those ribs heal without any trouble."

"I'll put up a coop for these pullets today. By the size of 'em, they should be layin' in two months or so. Haven't had an egg for purty nigh a year." He carried the box back to the stable.

"I bought them from a woman in town," said a voice behind her.

Megan whirled in surprise to see Steve at the top of the ladder.

"I've got a hankering for eggs myself." Slowly, carefully he climbed down and eased into a chair.

"You ought to be in bed," Megan scolded mildly. She felt an almost physical pain at the sight of his swollen, shiny, purple-splotched face.

"Never stayed in bed a day in my life." He drew in a quick breath. "I don't aim to start now."

"Breakfast will be ready soon." She peeked at the biscuits in the oven and sliced some bacon. The frying pan was sizzling and popping when Steve called her.

"Come here, Megan. Banjo brought in something I bought for you in town."

Megan checked the biscuits again, wiped her hands, and wonderingly obeyed.

"I thought you might like this." He held up a large bolt of cloth. "You look mighty fetching in blue."

Stunned, Megan reached out for the powder blue fabric. She rubbed her hand over the lacy white print.

"That was kind of you," she faltered, her cheeks pink.

"I got the whole bolt so you can make a real nice one."

Her steps were light as she carried the bolt into her room, sampling the smooth weave under hand as she went. In the bedroom she draped the end of the cloth over her shoulder and looked in the mirror nailed to her bedroom wall. That shade of blue was perfect for her hair and eyes. The roses in her cheeks and glow in her eyes added to the picture. With deft movements she smoothed the fabric around the bolt and put it into her trunk. Going back to the kitchen she avoided Steve's eyes as she passed, but inside she sang a soft, lilting, wordless melody.

Steve watched from the doorway when Megan took some scraps out to the dog after breakfast.

"I'm going to call him Lobo because he look like a wolf." The object of their attention bolted down a scrap of bacon and two biscuits. "Banjo told me he used to belong to Cunningham."

"He must have been living off of field mice," Steve remarked.

"I haven't been able to get near him, yet. It's taken six weeks for him to come this close."

Lobo sat on his haunches, watching Megan's face. He whined.

"All right, boy," she laughed, throwing him a third biscuit. "You always know when I'm holding out on you."

He picked up the biscuit and trotted off.

"That's it for the day. So far I've seen him only in the morning. He's getting braver because usually he won't come near the porch if he sees one of you men around."

"He'll be protection for you when Banjo and I have to be away. I'll be glad if you can get him tamed."

"I feel sorry for him. He's been all alone for over two years. I wonder how he survived the winters."

"Probably holed up in a cave somewhere." Steve walked back into to living room and eased down on the sofa. "Hand me my gunbelt, will you? I may as well clean my guns while I'm inside."

❧

It was early in August before Steve recovered enough to return to all his normal work. It took several days of painful practice to give him back his agility with a gun. Megan watched his recovery with mixed emotions. She was glad to see him strong again, but she knew each passing day brought closer another confrontation with the Harringtons. Someone was bound to be killed. Would it be Steve? She couldn't bear to voice the question even in her mind.

The hot summer seemed endless. Megan's face grew tan from long hours in the garden. She picked green beans until her arms and back groaned. She made catsup and chutney until the kitchen

cabinets could hold no more jars. This in addition to her weekly
chores of bread-making, butter-churning, and washing and ironing clothes made the days full indeed.

Late in the afternoons she often escaped the overheated house
by doing target practice with Steve. When he hurled glass bottles
into the air she could strike them four of five tries.

"You stay at it, and you'll soon be better than me," he said
one evening in mid-August. They were collecting guns and
shells to go inside. "I've never seen the like. Have you thought
of trying live game?"

"I don't think I could kill anything," she said, shaking her
head. "I couldn't stand to." They meandered in the direction of
the house.

"I would like to ride Candy," Megan said.

"We don't have a sidesaddle."

"I always rode astride when I was a girl. I can do the same
now. Would you teach me to saddle her?"

"A saddle may be too heavy for a little lady like you, but you
can try."

The saddle was heavy. The next day Megan gritted her teeth,
took a breath, and heaved. The leather hit the horse's back a bit
awry, but it stayed. Candy looked around and nuzzled Megan's
hand. Megan patted her nose.

"Don't worry, girl, we'll do it yet." She turned to Steve, smiling triumphantly. "Now what?"

"Make sure you didn't wrinkle the saddle blanket. Her back
will get sore if it's wrinkled." He lifted one edge of the saddle and
pulled the blanket. "Fasten the girth tightly." He firmly punched
the mare's stomach. "A canny horse will fill his belly with air, so
you can't tighten it right. Make 'em let it out before you cinch up.

"You can ride Billy or Star as well as Candy, but leave Caesar alone," he cautioned. "He's wild. He always tries to bite me
when I saddle him. Don't ever turn your back on him."

Megan grasped the pommel with her left hand and stepped into the stirrup. Mother's dark green riding habit fit her to perfection after she had sewn in a few tucks. Instead of the ribboned bowler that was supposed to complete the outfit, she wore a dark green bonnet. The feel of the saddle and the movements of the horse brought back the carefree fun she had known in Virginia. With Steve on Billy they cantered shoulder to shoulder in a circle around the meadow. When they got back to the yard Megan's cheeks were flushed, her eyes shone. She felt the exhilarating urgency of a six-month-old fawn on a crisp fall morning.

"Let's do it again," she begged, "only faster."

Steve laughed out loud at her childlike enthusiasm. Without answering, he urged Billy forward, leading out at a moderate gallop this time. Candy lengthened her stride and stayed beside Billy's right hindquarters until they reached the curve in the field; then she was shoulder to shoulder with him for the rest of the ride. Megan would have gone for a third round, but it was not to be. Practicality won out. Supper must be cooked and the hour was growing late.

After that day, Steve and Megan alternated riding and shooting in the late afternoons when they both were free. It was glorious to ride in the pine-scented air enjoying the country and their companionship. She was deeply in love with Colorado.

Often they rode south to the lake and strolled along its shore, charmed by a solitude that was interrupted only by an occasional bird call or the splash of a fat trout swimming under the surface. A thick grove of spruce blocked off everything but the sky. It seemed like she and Steve were the only people in the world when they were there.

"What was it like on the riverboats?" Megan asked one day as they rambled near the water's edge.

"At first it was exciting." Steve picked up a flat, smooth stone and skimmed it across the water. It hit three times and sank, leaving a spreading series of circles. "Bright lights, plush furnishings, elegantly dressed people." He glanced at her. "But when you probed beneath the surface, the picture wasn't nearly so appealing. It was there that I learned to use a hideout knife. It was that or risk being robbed every time I won a big stake." He selected another stone.

"Don't get me wrong. I enjoyed playing cards. It was intoxicating to be able to handle them and win." He shook his head. "But I learned those cards were a two-headed serpent. One bite and you were hooked. The second bite and they destroyed you." He flicked the stone with all his might. Five skips.

Megan watched his face as he spoke. It was the first time he had spoken of his past to her since they met in the hotel in Baltimore. This time she caught a better glimpse of the person behind his handsome face.

"I saw men destroyed too often. When I felt myself withering inside, I had to get out. That's why I don't play anymore, even for fun. I don't want to give the serpent a chance to bite me again."

The sun's slanted beams sifted across the treetops. Steve measured their angle with a quick look and pitched one last stone. "It's getting late," he said, reluctantly. "We'd best get back."

In the passing days, Megan learned to read his mood by the turn of his head or the movement of his hand. His smile made the day full of sunbeams; his deep, resonant voice touched an answering chord inside of her.

❧

"What is this?" Steve's clipped words, like stones thrown at a rock wall, brought Megan up short. She dumped the last pail of oats into Candy's trough and joined him beside the mare. He stood aside for her to see an ugly sore on Candy's back.

"You left a wrinkle in the saddle blanket." The hard set of his mouth condemned her.

"I was in a hurry to go riding with Susan when I saddled up." Megan avoided his eyes. Her tongue was suddenly thick and stupid. "I'm sorry."

He turned his back to her, folding the blanket with a snap.

She stroked the horse's neck. "I'm sorry, Candy. I didn't mean to hurt you. I'll be more careful after this." The horse lifted her head out of the feed trough to nuzzle Megan's shoulder. Megan rubbed the space between Candy's eyes. She gave the roan a loving pat and walked out of the stable.

"Megan." Steve called her back.

"Yes?" Reluctantly, she retraced her steps.

"I'm sorry I was hard on you." His mouth was still a thin, straight line, but his eyes were gentler than before.

"I shouldn't have been so careless. You were right about that." She met his eyes with a serious, steady gaze.

"Let's say we both fell short." The corners of his mouth turned up little. "Care to go for a walk after supper? I'd like to look over our garden before it gets dark."

"Sure. I'll put the kettle on now, so we can get an early start." She walked slowly to the house. It had been an unusual day, first a visit from Susan and now this interchange with Steve. Seeing that side of this personality was sobering and heartwarming at the same time.

❧

Susan Harrington's visits brought sweet relief to the tedium of those days. If Megan had a few hours free they would ride together. If not, Susan lent an extra pair of hands to Megan's never-ending chores.

"Everyone's going away for six weeks," Susan remarked later that week. They were sitting at the table shredding cabbage for sauerkraut. "Except me and three hands to watch over the ranch. All the hands are going on the cattle drive to Denver. It'll be a little lonely, but at least I'll have peace for a few days."

"You're always welcome here," Megan grinned, "especially if you keep helping with all these vegetables."

"You've had a rest from their harassment, too," Susan went on, "with the roundup last month and all." She emptied her pan of shredded cabbage into the large crock on the table and picked up another cabbage. "I wish Pa would stay so busy he'd forget this land." She pushed the damp tendrils from her forehead with the back of her wrist.

"Oh," Susan broke out excitedly, "I almost forgot to tell you. The Sanderses are having a dance on September twenty-fifth. Elaine told me last week when I saw her in town. You haven't met Elaine yet, have you?"

"Not yet." Megan poured more brine into the crock. "I don't get away much."

"I can't wait. I'm having a new dress made with a huge bustle and lots of ruffles."

Megan remembered the blue dress that hung half-finished in her closet. She had been so busy with the garden's harvest she hadn't been able to touch the dress for two weeks. With a few extra touches she could make it into a party dress. Maybe she could get some blue ribbon if Steve went into town soon. Plans for the party captured their attention and the basket of cabbage was finished in short order.

What good fun a frolic will be, Megan thought after Susan said good-bye and rode off. A party seemed especially exciting because she hadn't once been away from the ranch since they arrived three months before.

She drew the unfinished dress from the closet, caressing the soft fabric, and turning it critically in her hands. An extra ruffle here, some small embroidery there, and a little more fullness in the bustle. It would make a wonderful party dress. She held the dress under her chin and watched herself in the mirror, swaying gently to the music she could already hear.

The sound of horses in the yard shattered her daydream. She swept the dress back into the closet and scurried out to meet Steve and Banjo, back from a day of moving the longhorns to a new stretch of grass. Holding her skirt up, she ran lightly across the yard.

"Howdy, Miss Megan," Banjo said. His grin relaxed the tired lines around his mouth.

"What's got you so het up?" A faint grin hovered over Steve's features, a result of Megan's red cheeks and glowing eyes. "Who was here today?"

"Susan," Megan said, breathlessly. She stood near Steve as he dismounted. "The Sanderses are having a frolic. Elaine Sanders is putting it on." The words spilled out. "Everyone's going to be there. Can we go, Steve?"

Steve stopped short, soberly regarding her hopeful face. Without answering, he pulled Billy's reins to lead him into the stable.

"Steve?" Megan took a step after him.

"We'll talk it over in the house," Steve said tersely over his shoulder.

Crestfallen, Megan looked at Banjo who, carefully keeping his eyes on Kelsey, followed Steve into the stable.

Megan stood still a moment, staring at the empty stable doorway. She was confused and hurt. Search her mind as she might she could not understand Steve's reaction, nor Banjo's.

"About the frolic," Steve said after he had washed for supper. They were alone in the kitchen. "I'm not sure we ought to go." His voice was kind.

"Not go?" Disappointment fell on Megan with a thud. "Why not?"

Steve came near her, his face troubled. Megan had to lean her head back to look up at him he stood so close to her. She noticed his lined brow, his set jaw, and she rebelled.

"Please, Steve." She raised pleading eyes to meet his. "It would be so nice to have some fun after working so hard. It would do both of us good to forget the ranch for a few hours. It wouldn't hurt to go, would it? I do so want to go."

He ran his hand through his freshly combed hair, looked away, and looked back again.

"It's against my better judgment, Megan, but if you want to go that much, I guess we can." He looked deeply into her eyes, hesitated, and was gone.

nine

"I don't cotton to those parties much, Miss Megan," Banjo said to Megan's question the next morning. She had asked him to move a sack of chicken feed that had gotten wet on the bottom from a heavy rain the night before seeping under the stable wall and dampening the ground. "A frolic means dancin' and likker. As a Christian I can't approve of either one." His voice was mild, but his words carried conviction.

"I can't see why Miss Susan is so worked up about goin' over there anyways." He eased the sack of cracked corn to dry ground a few feet away. "Her pa and Sanders had words a year or so ago, and Jim Sanders is one to bear a grudge. When he first came to these parts, a man tried to push Sanders off'n his own range. Sanders killed him seven years later." He pushed his hat to the back of his head and glanced at Megan. "Oh, it was a fair fight all right. But Sanders had it in his craw the whole time. When men get their reason marred with drink things start happenin'. No good can come of it."

Megan could not understand his reasoning because she had many happy memories of lively music and excitement before the war. The balls her mother had given! Megan used to stay up long past her bedtime to peer under the stair railing, hypnotized by the colorful, laughing, dancing crowd below.

Banjo is old, she decided on her way to the house. *That must be it. He's too old to enjoy those things anymore.*

That evening, Steve's offer to take her to town with him the next day topped off her anticipation. Carefully counting her change, she mentally listed the things she would buy to complete her party costume.

The sky was cloudless, the sun strong on their ride to town. Megan raised her face and basked in the clear morning air. The tall, golden-tasseled stalks of corn hid the house from view before they were halfway around the meadow. Megan watched the curling morning glory vines along the edge of the field. They made a carpet on the ground and wound around the first stalks of every row. Steve had eyes only for the promising crop. If all went well, they would reap far more than he had estimated.

With the eagerness of a six-year-old planning for a birthday party, Megan visited the only milliner's shop in Juniper Junction. After a long session of lip biting and toe tapping, she finally purchased a blue silk bonnet with fluffy, white feathers on the left side tucked under the broad blue ribbon around the brim. Some extra ribbon for her dress was her next choice. As she was about to leave, a pair of long, white gloves caught her eye. She hesitated a moment, then impulsively nodded. Surely it wouldn't hurt to be a little daring. How many frolics would she get to out here in the wilderness? A thrill of expectancy passed through her as she gathered her parcels and stepped onto the boardwalk.

A letter was waiting for her at the post office. Impatient, she tore open the envelope the moment she was outside. Like a slow leak in a hot air balloon, her spirits sank. After two months, Jeremy was still the same: no worse, but no better. He was lonely for Megan, and would Megan please write him more often.

She stuffed the letter back into the envelope on her way to the hotel to join Steve for lunch. She tried to shake off her uneasiness and enjoy the rest of her special day, but the gloom clung to her, a nagging ache at the back of her mind.

A quiet dinner at the hotel, a trip to Harper's Emporium for supplies, and they started the long journey home. They had barely topped the first rise when a group of riders came toward them on the trail. The party was led by a tall, broad man wearing a large, white hat. He sat ramrod straight in the saddle with the unmistakable air of authority. The group split when they reached Chamberlin's buckboard, half on either side, and stopped. Each man except the leader was holding a weapon. Harrington's gun stayed in his holster.

"Chamberlin," the big man said, coldly, "you're a squatter. And you're more than that. You're a dirty rustler."

"I don't take that from any man." Steve's Winchester suddenly materialized in his hands.

"You'll take it from Victor Harrington." The big man's eyes narrowed. "I've lost a lot of stock ever since you moved on my land. Get out or you'll pay the piper."

"I already gave your son my answer. I haven't changed my mind."

Megan couldn't take her eyes off Victor Harrington sitting so arrogantly on his giant black horse. This was Susan's father.

"You'll go or I'll burn you out," Harrington persisted.

"I'll tell you this." Steve's knuckles were white on the rifle stock. He spat the words at his tormentor. "If you'd show a little backbone and stop hiding behind those toughs you ride with, I'd show you who you can run off. You probably haven't fought your own battles for years, Harrington. Are you afraid? We could settle it now, the two of us."

"I don't waste my time on vermin." Keeping his gaze straight ahead, Harrington prodded his horse. One by one his men followed.

Steve and Megan rode up the mountain in heavy silence. Megan secretly watched him. She was overwhelmed by the white hot temper she had witnessed, but at the same time she was glad Steve had talked straight to the big man. Harrington had trampled men under foot for twenty years. It was time someone stood up to him.

❧

As the frolic drew near, Megan pushed aside all thoughts of the

Harringtons. Daydreaming of lively music and pleasant conversation Megan stepped into the morning sunshine a week later. The glowing sun felt good after the chilly September evenings they were having. The stone house held the night coolness long into the day.

Humming softly, she took the feed pail from its peg and opened the sack of cracked corn. When she bent over the bag a strange, acrid smell made her draw back. She wrinkled her nose and peered down into the almost empty bag. Rolling down the top of the sack so she could see better she stirred the damp corn with the edge of the pail. A sticky film was over the grain.

Pulling her bottom lip between her teeth, she considered the unopened sack of feed Steve had bought on their last trip to town. He had told her to finish the old bag before using the new one. She'd better do as he said. He might be angry if she didn't. She scooped her pail into the corn and, holding it at arm's length, walked quickly to the hen yard. To her relief the six hens and two roosters attacked the feed with their usual energy.

Good, she thought. *If that's the case, why not give them the rest of the bag? Then it will be finished, and I won't have to handle the smelly stuff again.*

Holding it like an irritated mother holds a child's mud-covered shoes, she carried the offensive sack to the yard and shook it out. The greedy chickens scurried around clucking, fighting and scratching frantically.

The unpleasant job finished, she took the empty sack back to the stable. By the time she went into the henhouse to gather the eggs, her mind had wandered again to the upcoming frolic and the dress she had almost finished. Her imagination could already hear the music and the laughter-filled conversations. The henhouse became a ballroom and her gingham housedress was a elegant blue gown.

But when she returned to the henhouse door the sight of the

hen yard shocked her out of her fantasy.

One hen lolled her head from side to side and made a strange squeaking noise. Another walked in circles, her beak almost touching the ground. A rooster fluttered his wings and crowed, "Gobble-gobble-goo!"

Megan stared. She gasped when a hen fell to its side kicking convulsively.

"What did you feed them chickens, Miss Megan?" Banjo asked from the front of the stable. He propped a shoulder against the stable wall and looked on with interest, a smirk hovering about his face.

"What's wrong with them, Banjo?" she cried in alarm. She made a wide circle around the crazy chickens, watching them warily. "I gave them their corn a few minutes ago."

"That wet sack I moved for you a week or so ago?"

She nodded. Her dismay grew when the rooster flapped his wings for another crow and landed in a heap.

"They'll be all right by supper time." Banjo chuckled, softly.

"What's so funny?" she demanded, eyes flashing. "They might be poisoned. We could lose our eggs. I don't think that's anything to laugh about!"

"They're not poisoned." He chuckled at her indignation, and succeeded in fueling it further. "They're drunk. Ever hear of corn likker? Home brew?"

"Drunk?"

Cluck-clucking, a hen walked head-on into the henhouse wall.

Megan's face was pink, her ears were hot, and she could hardly speak.

"This'll be a whopper of a story, Miss Megan," Banjo said, grinning widely and shaking his head. "A real whopper."

"Don't tell Steve," she begged, putting her hand on his arm. "Please, Banjo!"

"Don't tell Steve what?" a familiar voice asked.

She whirled around and there was Steve, his expression an

identical twin to Banjo's. Face flaming, she looked from Steve's grin to Banjo's poorly muffled laughter and back again. Without another word she did an about-face and marched to the house, her head held high and her back board straight.

She couldn't bear to look at either of them that night at supper. The thought of what she had done set her cheeks on fire. Both men were on their best behavior. They seemed completely unaware of her lingering embarrassment. By the time she served their after-dinner coffee she was ready to believe they had forgotten all about the chickens. She breathed still easier when they rose to do the evening choring.

"Do me a favor, will you, Megan?" Steve said before following Banjo. His hand was on the latch as though he had almost forgotten to tell her something.

"Yes?" Puzzled, she looked at him. His face was expressionless except for the smallest hint of a twinkle.

"Don't ever feed the horses." With a friendly, teasing smile he closed the door quickly behind him.

Her first impulse was to fling her coffee cup after him, but her temper quickly dwindled.

"He couldn't resist," she said aloud, chuckling. For some obscure reason she kept feeling an urge to laugh as she cleared away the supper dishes that evening.

❧

The day of the frolic dawned dark and foreboding with the promise of heavy rain. With growing chagrin, Megan watched the sky. She hoped the rain would come and be done before too late in the day. She fairly skimmed through her housework that morning, wishing away the hours until time to dress, for her party gown hung in her room begging her to hurry.

With many anxious glances at the sky, she cleared away the lunch dishes and prepared to take a short nap. The dark clouds continued billowing in growing mounds, swirling menacingly. Still it did not rain.

At last the hour arrived. Megan slid into the light blue swirl of ruffles, ribbons, and lace she had spent so many hours preparing. She set to work brushing her hair into a stylish chignon she had seen in Susan's copy of *Harper's* magazine. Frowning first in concentration, then in frustration, she rested her tired arms a moment and wondered if she would ever get it right. At last, she slowly turned in front of her small mirror, satisfied.

Steve rose from his chair as the rustle of her skirt and gentle tapping of her shoes announced her arrival in the living room. His gaze lifted slowly from the wide ruffle brushing the floor in front and drawing up to join the cascade of ruffles descending from the bustle at her back, up, up to the halo of wispy ringlets that circled her face, and beyond to her rosy cheeks and starry eyes, devouring her face with his eyes. Megan was captivated by the power of his gaze. How long they stood motionless, she did not know. Suddenly, he looked down at his hat, held firmly in his hand. When he looked up his expression was closed, the same expressionless mask he wore so often these days except perhaps a little softened.

"Ready?" he asked, politely.

"Yes." She pulled her mother's white silk shawl over her arm, and swished through the door he opened for her.

ten

High above the horizon the sun peeked through a crack in the dark cloud cover when Steve and Megan left the ranch. Steve had placed a piece of tarpaulin in the back of the wagon to cover them in case it rained in earnest. Occasionally a drop fell on Megan's hand or face, and she looked anxiously at the black, billowing mass overhead, but it did not rain.

A carriage and two buckboards stood outside the Sanderses' barn when they arrived. Smiling excitedly, Susan was framed in the wide doorway when they pulled to a halt under a spreading cottonwood tree. She was lovely in a flowing, lacy, yellow gown that brought out the highlights in her strawberry blond hair.

"Megan," Susan called when they reached the door, "I'm so glad you came a little early. I want you to meet Elaine. You won't mind, will you, Mr. Chamberlin?" Assuming Steve's consent, she led Megan to the makeshift cloakroom and waited impatiently while Megan hung up her wrap and checked her hair. "There she is." Susan pointed toward a dark-haired young woman with olive skin who stood talking to a young man on the other side of the carefully swept barn. Elaine was petite and fine-featured, almost like a china doll.

After the quick introduction, Elaine said, "If we get a chance," she lowered her voice conspiratorially, "we must escape to the house for a chat. It's been ages since I've seen another woman."

"Elaine!" a man's voice called from the direction of the musicians.

"That's Ernie. He's one of the fiddlers." She put her hand on her silk skirt and lifted it slightly. "If you need anything just yell, Elaine!" With a tinkling laugh she hurried away.

"Elaine's a world of fun," Susan declared. One of the fiddlers drew his bow across the strings. "They're getting ready to start. I'll see you later."

Working her way back to Steve's side, Megan wound her way through the milling crowd that had gathered since her arrival. She smiled and nodded a greeting to several people she recognized: Kip Morgan who had been with them on the stage, Wyatt Hammond, Banjo's friend, and Mr. Harper who bobbed his head absently in response to Mrs. Pleurd's chatter. Victor Harrington planted himself near the door, his henchmen nearby. The Hohner boys, Henry and Al, lounged near the refreshment table. They gawked openly at the young women, nudging each other in the ribs from time to time. Megan looked away when she passed them. Something about them made her feel unclean.

"I'm not much of a dancer," Steve said when she reached him, "but I'm willing to try if you are." Taking her hand and placing it on his bent arm, he led her to the dance floor to join the square dance that was setting up.

"I thought you said you rode the riverboats," Megan countered with a smile, "and you don't dance?" They were waiting hand in hand for the beginning chord.

"I stuck to the tables." He looked down at her with a teasing grin. "I always considered women to be trouble." His grin widened at her surprised expression, and they fell in step with the music.

"Swing your partner, the caller chanted, and they danced and danced until Megan's head reeled.

"I'd like to sit down," she said when there was a break in the music. "I'm a little tired."

"Having a good time?" Steve asked, handing her a cup of grape punch.

"Wonderful! I don't know when I've had so much fun." Still under the spell of the music, she sipped her punch and watched the dancers.

"I believe I'll check the horses."

Megan nodded to him, preoccupied with the scene before her.

A deep, prolonged boom of thunder, almost like a drum roll, interrupted the gay music. In minutes, the deluge of rain hammering on the barn roof gave the fiddler competition.

"Let it pour," a man standing near her said loudly to his companion. "We can sure use it."

And pour it did. The roar on the roof made it impossible to continue the dancing. The music could scarcely be heard. For fifteen minutes it lasted until, as suddenly as it began, the rain stopped and the frolic resumed its breathtaking pace.

After a while it occurred to Megan that Steve had been away a long time. She was strolling leisurely in the direction of the door when he suddenly appeared through the crowd.

"I was beginning to wonder what became of you." Her smile froze when a woman's piercing scream shattered the gay atmosphere. Following Steve's gaze, she saw the cause of the confusion, and darkness closed in on her. For an instant she was afraid she would faint. Steve's strong arm was around her instantly, and she clung to him.

Outside the open door lay the body of a huge man. A knife was buried up to the long, black haft into the left side of his back. His out-flung hand gripped the door jamb. Megan, transfixed, stared at that strong, calloused hand. She saw it slowly relax its grip and fall limp. Horror swept over her in great, crashing waves. She buried her face in the rough cloth of Steve's coat.

"It's Harrington," a man's voice called. "Victor Harrington."

"He's pulled leather," another voice added grimly.

"Get hold of yourself, Megan." Steve pulled her away from him and looked into her face. "Susan is going to need someone. He's her pa."

Megan drew a shaky breath and turned her face away from the scene in the doorway. She knew he was right. She ought to find Susan.

"Pa!" Susan's anguished, hysterical cry struck an answering

chord in Megan. Her own feelings forgotten, she rushed to her friend's side.

Susan's face was white as chalk; her eyes were wide with terror. She stared dazedly at the body of her father.

Megan put her arms around the shaking young woman and pulled her away.

"Come," Elaine said softly in her ear, "bring her to the house."

Together Megan and Elaine half-carried the grief-stricken woman into the Sanderses' living room, and Elaine ran to the kitchen for some strong, sweet tea.

"Pa," Susan groaned between deep, body-shaking sobs.

Megan stroked her hand and tried to find something consoling to say. But she felt totally helpless. Nothing would bring Susan's father back. A hot, choking sob welled up in Megan's breast. She held it down, but it grew until it fairly smothered her. She understood Susan's loss. Hadn't she lost both father and mother as Susan had? What comfort was there?

None, her soul cried out. *No comfort. No comfort anywhere.*

She sat with Susan, hardly moving or speaking until Beau Harrington's slurred speech rose to a shout outside the Sanderses' door. It was past midnight.

"I want to see Susan!"

"Your sister is sleeping," Ruth Sanders, Elaine's mother, answered flatly.

Megan drew aside the curtain a fraction of an inch to see Mrs. Sanders barring Beau from coming up the porch stairs. Even from the ground the young man was taller than the little woman, but she seemed to tower over him, so great was the strength of her determination.

"She was hysterical," Elaine's mother continued, "so I gave her a little laudanum to calm her. She'll sleep for a long while. Why don't you leave her here tonight?"

Beau blinked stupidly at the commanding figure before him, apparently deciding his next course of action.

"Megan Chamberlin is with her now." Ruth Sanders took a

step forward as though to force him back.

"Chamberlin!" He bristled, spitting out the words. "Don't you let any of that lowdown, murderin' bunch near Susan." He clenched his fists. "You get that squatter's wife out of there, or I'll bust in and take Susan home now." He scowled threateningly.

"How dare you say such a thing!"

"It was her husband killed my pa," Beau insisted. "He wanted revenge for Pa trying to run him off."

Megan moved away from the window and sank into a chair. Leaning her throbbing head against the high back, she closed her eyes.

"You're drunk." Megan clearly heard Ruth Sanders's disdainful voice. "Go somewhere and sleep it off, or I'll have to call Jim from the barn."

Boots crunching on gravel was all the answer she received. Megan opened her eyes when she heard the front door open. Mrs. Sanders paused when she caught sight of Megan in the front room before deliberately closing and locking the front door. Even at this late hour, Mrs. Sanders showed no signs of strain or fatigue.

"You heard what he said?" she asked softly, coming near Megan.

Mutely, Megan nodded. After the strain of the evening, Beau's accusation was more than she could endure.

"You may as well know. Clyde Turner, Harrington's foreman, said he saw your husband outside right before the murder, and he knows your husband is good with a knife."

Megan pressed her temples.

"There wasn't enough evidence to pin Harrington's murder on your husband for sure, but there was quite a bit of arguing out there." She patted Megan's shoulder. "I'm sorry. You're new out here, and you'll have to get used to our ways. The law is a long way off in Denver, so the men have to settle these things themselves mostly. But with it being outright murder, they'll probably call in the U.S. Marshal to investigate if he has time.

"Your husband's been waiting with the buckboard for over an hour. You're done in. Maybe you'd best go on home. We'll see to Susan."

Megan sat in silence for a long moment.

"Please tell Susan I'll do anything I can to help her if she needs me," she managed at last, getting shakily to her feet.

Steve was at her side the instant she stepped off the porch. He draped her shawl about her and handed her her bonnet. Helping her into the buckboard, he clucked to the horses as he gathered the reins, and they were off into the moonlight.

When the trees had closed around them, shielding them from the watching eyes of those still at the Sanderses' ranch, Megan's control disintegrated. She sobbed into her handkerchief, her shoulders heaving with every breath. Steve put his arm about her, but she barely noticed. The sympathetic moon drew a lacy cloud handkerchief across its face, darkening the night to hide her tears.

"It's all my fault," she murmured in an agony of self-reproach.

"What's your fault?" Steve demanded.

"I. . .I shouldn't have insisted on going to the. . .to the frolic." She sniffled, wadding her soggy handkerchief. "If we hadn't gone they couldn't have accused you of. . .of. . . ." A fresh storm of tears broke out.

"Wait a minute." His voice was stern. "Wait a minute. They could accuse me of coming around without attending the party, you know. Harrington was killed outside, remember. Someone could have been lurking in the darkness unbeknownst to anyone." He looked at her intently through a fresh stream of moonlight as the cloud covering passed on. "Who's been telling you things?"

"Mrs. Sanders."

Steve's gruff tone had calmed her emotional tempest somewhat. She stared at her hands, not wanting to meet his eyes, aware of the solid strength of his arm and stiffness of his coat against her shoulder. Stumbling and groping for words, she told him of her conversation with Ruth Sanders.

"In the first place," Steve said quietly when she was through,

"Turner didn't make a direct accusation. He made some pointed hints, and I'm sure every man there knew what he was getting at, but they're not going to string me up on that basis.

"As a matter fact, I'm glad we were there. I had a chance to look around a bit after you left with Susan. I saw a few things that could mean somethin'." He reached inside his coat and handed her his handkerchief. "Here, take mine. Looks like yours is pretty used up."

Meekly, Megan wiped her face. She was a little ashamed of her outburst now. She felt herself relaxing as she listened to his calm voice, and she drew strength from his strength.

"It was a thrown knife," he was saying. "I went to the door after you went out with Susan. The downpour had wiped out all the footprints of people arriving. Harrington's prints were the only ones coming across the clearing in front of the barn. At one spot he stumbled. I figure that's where he was nailed. No one could have been close enough to reach him there."

"You can tell all that?"

"I learned many useful things in the Army of the Confed'racy, Miss Megan," he said, lightly. "I also located some boot prints under the shelter near the hitching rail. It had a star design in the heel. Looked like brand new boots to me." Growing animated, he said, "Harrington's back would have been toward that person as he crossed the clearing, too. It seems pretty simple to me. Find out who's knife slick and wears those boots, and we'll have the murderer."

"Did you tell the men what you saw?" Megan held her shawl closely around her. She had begun to shiver.

"They weren't over-anxious to listen to anything I had to say," he admitted, reluctantly. "They don't know for sure I'm guilty, but they don't know for sure I'm not. And I'm a stranger. That's ten counts against me to start out." He paused, guiding the horses over the bank of the stream that circled the lower meadow.

"Try not to worry, Megan," he said after they were across. His voice was tender.

eleven

Banjo was standing in the open doorway of the stable when they rode into the yard.

"Evenin', folks." He took the reins from Steve. "I'll tend the horses."

"We had some trouble," Steve said after he had helped Megan down. "Victor Harrington was murdered tonight. Stabbed in the back."

Banjo whistled softly. "You don't say. Any idea who did it?"

"Steve was accused," Megan blurted out. "Folks don't know whether to believe it or not."

"I found a couple o' clues." Steve told Banjo of his finds.

"Believe I'll ride over that way come daylight." Banjo rubbed his chin. "I'm a fair hand at readin' signs. Maybe I can come up with somethin' more."

&

The sun shone full in Megan's face when she opened her eyes the next morning. She blinked and sat up, disgruntled at having slept so late. This, along with the heavy feeling in her head and limbs, did nothing for her disposition. She put a weak hand to her head and pressed her eyes tightly closed. The terrors of the evening before rushed over her.

She ached afresh for Susan, left alone now to cope with her explosive brother. Megan hoped Susan wouldn't believe Steve was guilty of killing her father. How could she bear to lose Susan's friendship? She had come to love Susan like a sister.

Steve was not in the house when Megan came out of her room. She didn't feel like eating. Instead she went out to her favorite haunt at the eastern side of the house. She walked off the porch to sit in the grass and look out at the rolling hills. She had been there for half an hour enjoying the breeze and the quietness of the landscape when she was startled by a stealthy movement beside her.

It was Lobo. He was lying about six feet away with his head on his paws, watching her.

"I forgot to feed you this morning, didn't I? I'm sorry, Lobo. I guess I had a lot on my mind this morning. Will you stay here if I go in for something?" She stretched her hand out toward the shaggy head. He didn't shy away. Edging a little closer, she let him sniff her hand without trying to touch him. "Wait here."

Moving quietly to keep from scaring him, she went inside and hurried back with a scrap of corn bread and a small dish of cold, congealed gravy.

She stood nearby while Lobo gobbled down the food. This time, instead of rushing away, he came to her and licked her hand. Megan knelt down in front of him. His gray face turned up to her face, his tail gave a short wag.

"Are you ready to be friends, Lobo?" she whispered. "I won't hurt you, you know." Gently, she touched his scruffy head, rubbing between his ears and long neck. "I'd like you to stay here with me and not run away every day. I'm lonely like you." She talked to him about Jeremy and how she hoped he would come to Colorado to be with them, stroking the dog all the while. His ears were pricked up, and his eyes followed her face. If she hadn't known better, she would have declared he understood every word.

They were still deep in conversation when Kelsey's lop-eared head appeared on the trail. Megan watched Banjo's progress around the meadow. When he came close, Lobo gave one short, sharp bark and ran away. Steve walked slowly from the corral to join them.

"Found a few things you'd be interested in," Banjo said, stepping from the saddle.

Steve stood without expression, waiting. Megan impatiently clenched her apron. Banjo seemed in no hurry. He ground hitched Kelsey and slowly perched on the edge of the porch.

"I found those boot marks you mentioned." He knocked his

hat to the back of his head. "That feller stood there a while like he was waitin' for somethin'. The ground was tramped down a good bit with his boot prints. He was wearing California spurs. The big rowels gouged into the dirt a couple o' times. He's about six feet tall judging from his stride."

He reached into his shirt pocket.

"I found somethin' else interestin'." He stretched his hand out to Steve, a small piece of wood in the palm. "Looks to me like the man we want has a habit of chewin' short, green juniper twigs with the bark peeled off. I found two o' these. Juniper has a powerful taste. Don't care for it myself, but this hombre must have a likin' for it."

Steve turned the twig in his hand, studying it thoughtfully.

"I talked with Ruth Sanders a while this mornin'," Banjo continued. "The funeral is gonna be tomorrow at the Rockin' H. One of Harrington's hands went to Denver to get a parson. There's no parson in Juniper. A circuit ridin' preacher comes by ever' three months or so, but he's not due for another month." He accepted the twig that Steve returned to him. "What I was thinkin' on was this. If Miss Megan would like to go to this here funeral on account of bein' Miss Susan's friend, I'd be willin' to go along. That is if it's all right with you, Chamberlin."

"Megan?" Steve put the question to her.

"I'd like to go, Banjo. How is Susan? Did Mrs. Sanders say?"

"She's still with the Sanderses. Will be until the funeral. Miss Ruth says she's real quiet. Won't hardly talk to nobody, even Miss Elaine." He shook his head sadly. "I'm real sorry for the poor thing."

Megan climbed the porch steps with a tired tread. She put some soup on the stove to boil and went out back to the clothes she'd left soaking in the big tub overnight. She scrubbed and rubbed, squeezed and rinsed, puzzling over the clues Banjo had found, but her foggy mind could not make any sense out of them.

❦

When Megan came outside after breakfast the next morning Lobo was lying on the ground beside the porch steps watching the door. Wagging his matted tail, he stood up and met her at the bottom step.

"Here you go. Some bones from last night's supper. If you had come last night you wouldn't have had to wait until now to get them."

The dog settled in for a long, ecstatic gnawing session.

"I've got to go out, so I can't stay to talk," she continued. "I wish you'd stay around."

He raised his head, swished his tail, and gave a short bark.

Megan laughed. "So, you're talking back to me now. We're making progress."

Megan and Banjo set out after lunch. Megan's stomach was in knots. Not only did she dread the funeral itself, but she wasn't sure how Susan would act when she saw her. Megan's face was ghostly pale against the severe black broadcloth of her dress and bonnet, the same ones she had worn to mourn her mother.

The service had barely started when they arrived. Crude benches had been set up in the yard beneath a dozen tall aspens. A slight breeze caused a faint whispering rustle among the leaves. The shiny, black coffin, a wreath of yellow flowers on the lid, was at the front. A short man with a dark complexion and a large, hook nose stood behind the coffin, a black book open in his hand.

Banjo led Megan to a seat in the rear. Without turning her head, Megan looked over the grieving congregation. Susan, darkly veiled, sat with Beau near the front. Megan could see Susan trembling even at a distance. Beau looked straight ahead like a statue, oblivious of his sister's suffering.

The minister's high-pitched nasal voice droned on and on. Megan scarcely heard what he said, so caught up was she with the violence of her own emotions. The grim congregation, the coffin, and the minister reminded her with brutal clearness of her own bereavement. She wept soundlessly, without trying to stop her tears. Occasionally she dabbed at her cheeks with a black, lace-edged handkerchief. She wept for Susan, for her own tragedies, for the feeling of utter hopelessness she felt in her soul. The parson's words were eloquent, but she found no relief in his message.

At last, the assembly moved en masse to the grave site where the minister said a prayer and threw a handful of dirt on the lowered coffin. By twos and threes the mourners left the grave. From a cool distance they bowed in Megan's direction and nodded to Banjo, eyes averted. Susan, one of the last to leave, raised her head when she caught sight of Megan. She hesitated, glanced at Beau's back as he walked toward the house, and came over to grasp Megan's clenched hands in her icy, trembling ones.

Through the black veil Megan could see Susan's hollow, red-rimmed eyes and gaunt cheeks.

"I'm so glad you came, Megan," Susan whispered quickly. A smoldering fire burned from within her. Megan glimpsed it as she leaned forward. "I don't care what they say. I don't think Steve did it."

Tears streamed afresh down Megan's face. She couldn't speak.

"I'll be over when I can." A quick squeeze of her hand and she hurried to catch up to her brother.

Banjo took Megan's arm and walked with her to the buckboard. She couldn't stop crying. On the seat of the buckboard she held her handkerchief over her mouth and bowed her head until her face was all but hidden by the brim of her bonnet. Banjo called to the horses, and they set off.

"Miss Megan, Jesus would carry the load for you if you would let Him," Banjo said after several minutes had trudged heavily by.

"How could He help me?" she asked, looking up. Her eyes were red and swollen. Her chin quivered.

"Jesus said, 'Come unto me, all ye that labour and are heavy laden, and I will give you rest.' If you know you are a sinner and need Him to wash your sins away, He'll save you. The choice is as simple as that.

"I know there's plenty o' highfalutin' preachers who would like to make it seem harder than it is, but God's love is available to everyone. Even a child can understand it. God doesn't force His love on anyone. He lets each person choose for himself."

"How do I come?"

"Just pray and tell Him you mean business. Tell Him you know what you are and you want to claim His blood to wash your sins away. You know He died on the cross for you, don't you?"

"Of course." She remembered the camp meetings she had attended long ago in Virginia. The fiery preaching had made a lasting impression.

Was she a sinner? She didn't have to think about it long before she had to admit she was. She knew she had blamed God for her problems. She had never tried to live her life to please Him.

"Remember, God loves you," Banjo said, softly. "He wants to help you."

Megan squeezed her eyes shut. She poured out her tortured soul before the Almighty. There was no lightning bolt, no crash of thunder, no audible voice from heaven, yet surely, definitely, Jesus calmed the churning, frothing sea that was inside her. Some sadness still lingered, but for the first time in her life she was at peace.

"I did it, Banjo," she said softly when she looked up. "And God heard me. I know He did. I feel so quiet inside." She gazed into the distance examining the change within her like a mother examines her newborn child.

"That's the peace of God," Banjo said, nodding. "It's one of the greatest blessings of being a Christian. As long as you obey Him, that peace will stay with you.

"Do you have a Bible?" he asked.

"Yes. I have one in my trunk." She thought of the old black Bible that had been a gift to her father from a beloved teacher. How glad she was she had brought it along.

"Read it every day," Banjo advised. "You'll get strength from it."

"I will read it," she promised. "I surely will."

And read she did. The words in that old Bible came alive as she read each morning, often before dawn. She grew to love its delicate ivory pages. It was marvelous the way its message met her heart's need every time. She never forgot the day she found the verse in 1 Peter, "Casting all your care upon him, for he careth for you." Knowing God cared for her gave her new strength.

It was well she had found new strength, for only a week later Banjo brought her a letter that caused her to cry out for still more.

twelve

The letter read:

> *Dear Megan,*
>   *I thought you should know Jeremy is having a
> time of it. The doctor says he has to go back to
> his bed agin. His heart does git to racing when he
> sits up a while. I visit him every day but he misses
> you powerful. He loves your letters. Reads 'em
> till he has 'em down by heart.*
>
>   *Love,*
>   *Em*

Megan sat on the edge of her bed, rereading the letter. How bad Jeremy really was she couldn't tell. She felt sick with longing to be with him, to hold him close and tell him she loved him. She knelt by the big bed and rested her head on the quilt to give her fears and heartaches to the One Who had promised to care for her. An hour later a tender, sweet calmness replaced the fear and anguish. She washed the tears from her cheeks. Surely God would take care of Jeremy.

An idea came clearly as she patted her face dry with a towel. Jeremy had never heard that he could have his sins forgiven. She must write to him immediately and tell him about how she had found Jesus. And Em, yes, Em.

The letter was hard to begin, but once she found a starting place, her pen flew. There was so much to share of the joy and peace she had found and wished for her loved ones to find, also. Jesus was the answer to their devastating loss. He gave hope, blessed hope.

The letter was lying on top of her trunk ready for mailing the next morning when she went out to the henhouse. Steve and Banjo were working frantically to get the corn crop harvested for fear of a frost destroying it. When she finished her chores she would help pick the fat ears while the men chopped the stalks for cattle feed.

The sound of the birds twittering in the branches of the oaks, the soft breeze flowing down from the mountain, even the familiar barnyard smells of earth and straw lifted her spirits. Something brushed against her skirt making her turn around. It was Lobo walking behind her.

"Well hello." Megan knelt down to rub his neck. He leaned into her hand a little, his head cocked to one side. "I hate to tell you this but you do need a bath. I wonder what color you really are under all that dirt." She stood up. "I have to hurry. Steve needs me to help get in the corn." She continued across the yard, followed by Lobo. He went into the stable with her while she drew a pail of grain from the burlap sack.

"Chook! Chook! Chook!" she called to the clucking, scratching hens while she threw handfuls of cracked corn to the ground. Suddenly she stopped in midmotion, staring at the side of the stable, the side not seen from the house. Scrawled on the weathered gray boards in large, white letters was one word: MURDERER.

For a full ten seconds she stood there. She clenched her fists, pressing her lips so tightly they were all but invisible. Beau Harrington! It had to be Beau Harrington who did such a ghastly thing! She glared at the wall as though it were a living thing mocking her, mocking Steve, mocking their cause. Hadn't they done only what was right? Wasn't Victor Harrington wrong in trying to force them away? The pail of corn fell to the ground, forgotten.

"Well," she fumed, "he won't have the satisfaction of upsetting Steve with his malicious pranks. I'll scrub that wall before he sees it."

Shuffling her way through the mob of chickens looting the pail at her feet, she went through the rear door of the stable to fill a pail with water and get a broom. She scoured ferociously, until the whitewash was nothing more than a gray smear.

Satisfied, she retrieved her empty feed pail and walked slowly to the corral to give Candy the carrot in her apron pocket and rest a minute to calm her shaken nerves. It wasn't until she got back to the house that she realized Lobo still followed her.

"Here, Lobo," she called holding out her hand. He trotted up and licked her hand. "You're a good fella." She scratched the ruff behind his neck. "Steve's probably wondering what became of me." She gave him a parting pat and then scurried inside to get a lunch packed and put on her bonnet.

After dark that evening the men had barely reached the house to wash up for supper, when a wide, powerfully built man cantered in. He had a square face with a thick neck that seemed to be one with his wide chest. His silver badge reflected the lamplight streaming from the open doorway.

"Evenin', gentlemen," he said, holding his reins loosely on the pommel. "Is one of you Steve Chamberlin?"

"I am." Steve stepped forward from the porch. "What can I do for you?"

"I'm Ben Walker, the U.S. Marshal. I'd like to ask you a few questions."

"Certainly. Come in and set a spell. We were just about to sit up to the table. You're welcome to join us."

"I'd be much obliged." The lawman dismounted. "Don't get much chance to eat home cooking in my business."

Megan, watching from the door, couldn't believe Steve's unconcern. How could he act so naturally when the marshal could be here to arrest him? She clasped her hands tightly together across her waist.

"We've a guest for supper, Megan," Steve called. "Set another place."

The fork and knife rattled against the enamel plate as Megan set them down. Taking a deep breath and biting her lip, she willed herself to calm down. Quickly, she set out a jar of her own bread-and-butter pickles for good measure.

"This is my wife, Megan," Steve said when they came inside.

"Ma'am." Walker took off his big hat and offered a polite smile.

"Hello." She smiled, but her cheeks felt stiff and heavy.

The man wearing the silver star was generous in his praise of the steaks and new potatoes baked with butter. He also commented on the bread while he was buttering his third piece.

"You're a blessed man, Chamberlin," he said, pushing back his chair. "I haven't had a finer meal in a coon's age."

Steve gave Megan that slow smile that made her glow inside. "I can't but agree with you, Mr. Walker," he said.

"What's on your mind?" Steve asked when the men were seated in the living room around the crackling fire. Megan, still clearing away the dishes, strained her ears to hear. Her hands moved automatically, for her mind was far from the chore at hand.

"I'm investigating the Harrington murder. I'm sure you know you've been accused in so many words. I must say there doesn't seem to be an overabundance of evidence against you, but four different people have told me you're an ace with a knife. I thought I'd come out and see what you had to say."

"I'll tell you all I know," Steve said, easily. "Banjo can tell you some, too. He picked up some signs over at the Running M."

"What was your relationship to Harrington?"

Systematically, the marshal directed the questions until the entire story was told. Megan finished the dishes and quietly joined the men in the living room.

"What's your opinion of the folks around here, Banjo?" the marshal continued. "You've been in these parts long enough to know the lay of the land. Being from Denver puts me at a disadvantage. Who had a grudge against Harrington?"

"Most folks hereabouts," Banjo said after considering a minute or two. "Harrington pushed folks around to suit him. Offhand I'd say Jim Sanders, because of an old dispute, and Wyatt Hammond, because of Harrington's daughter. Then there's Logan Hohner, one of the blacksmiths in town. German man with two grown, no-account sons. He has a rawhide outfit north of here."

"What was Harrington's beef with him?" Walker asked.

"Accused him of rustlin'."

"He had a real imagination about rustlers, didn't he?" Steve asked quickly. "That's what he accused me of on the trail."

"I guess he's been losing cattle for four, five years from what Wyatt tells me. Never has been able to catch the rascals," Banjo said. His chair creaked as he changed position. "Then there's his son.

"I have my doubts Beau would have the gumption to do it, but he sure is a rebellious one. He could have gotten impatient to have the reins on the Rocking H himself." He paused. "I'm talking through my hat, Mr. Walker. I don't have any proof for that."

"I'm not saying I'm sorry Harrington's out of the picture," Steve admitted. "But I think it could have been handled better. You know, a fair fight. Whoever did it is a coyote. Not fit to live among decent folk."

It was late when the marshal left. Banjo went on to the stable when the big man rode away.

"Do you think Walker believes you did it?" Megan asked, anxiously.

"Can't say for sure." Steve sat on a chair near her. "All we can do is wait for his decision. But he did say he'd be interested to hear of anything else we may learn in the meantime." He leaned slightly toward Megan. "I don't want you to make yourself sick by worrying over this thing. When a man's in the right he shouldn't have anything to fear. Folks hereabouts are basically honest. They don't want to punish the wrong man any more than you or I do."

"It's hard not to worry, though." Megan looked down at her hands folded tightly in her lap. "There's so much at stake."

"You've been a real trooper, Megan. I'm glad you were the one I brought out here with me."

Megan glanced at him. He was watching her closely. She felt her face warm.

"I believe God will work everything out for the best." She wanted to tell him about her new faith but wasn't sure how to go about it.

"God?" Steve's eyebrows rose higher.

"I trusted Jesus as my Savior a few days ago." Once she had found an opening she spoke with assurance. "The Bible says that He will give rest to people who carry heavy burdens. Since I trusted Him, I know there's a difference. You may not be able to see it outside, but I know it's there deep inside."

"If that makes you feel better, I'm all for it," he said, awkwardly.

"Have you thought much about God?"

"Not much." He slammed the door on that subject and opened another. "The corn crop is excellent," he said abruptly. "I'm sure I'll be able to make four or five times what I spent for seed. If the frost holds off tonight, we'll finish getting it in tomorrow, and I'll take it to the mill the next day."

"I hope the other people around here don't convince the marshal you're guilty," she returned to the subject uppermost in her mind.

"I'm not worried about that." Steve relaxed, stretching his legs in front of him. "There is something that does bother me, though."

"What?"

"I've never held a knife around anyone in Colorado to my knowledge, except Banjo and you." He looked at his boots thoughtfully, pursing his lips.

"So?" His silence was maddening.

"So how does everyone know that I can handle one?"

thirteen

October days were busy indeed. With Lobo trailing after her like a gray shadow, Megan followed the buckboard through the woods, picking up deadfall to fuel the stove and fireplace through the winter. Banjo butchered a fat, young cow, and showed them how to jerk the beef and store it for the time when game was scarce.

Megan continued her target practice though her rides with Steve became less frequent. There simply wasn't time for both.

She held her rifle by the stock and gave it an excited shake the day she overlapped three shots in the center of a tin can lid at two hundred feet. Steve chuckled and shook his head when he retrieved the lid and examined it.

"I haven't seen many men who could do that," he said, giving her a wide approving grin. She glowed under his praise.

Megan had conflicting emotions the day she watched Susan's boyish figure ride in. She was glad to see her friend, but she dreaded hearing the news Susan carried. Megan lay the heavy iron on the kitchen stove, hung up the shirt she had been ironing, and went out to greet her.

"Morning!" Megan called with a cheerfulness she didn't feel.

Susan waved a greeting and ground hitched the chestnut on the edge of the meadow where he could reach the rich grass, and came to the house. She seemed like a vacant shell of the vivacious, quick-smiling young woman she had been such a short time ago. Always slender, she was now gossamer-thin and pale to the lips.

"I had to get away from the ranch for a while," she said when they sat down. "I had to talk to somebody." Her face contorted, and Megan was afraid she was going to cry.

"I've been missing you, too," Megan said, trying to ease the tension.

"I'm so worried. I haven't been able to sleep or eat much the past two weeks. It's about Wyatt." Tears spilled over her cheeks and fell to her shirt. She pulled a handkerchief from her pocket and pressed it against her face. Her sobs were soundless but they came from deep inside.

Megan didn't know what to say.

"Tell me about Wyatt," Megan prompted when the other woman's sobs had almost subsided. "You never have, you know."

Susan looked up from behind her handkerchief. "How do you know about Wyatt?"

"Banjo told me."

"Oh." Susan wiped her eyes. "That's right, Banjo would know." She drew a shaky breath, and kept her eyes on her fingers twisting and wadding her wet, wrinkled handkerchief. "There's not that much to tell, really. He came to work at the ranch about two years ago. He works Pa's horses." She cleared her throat. "I like to ride, and I spend quite a lot of time at the stable. One thing led to another, and. . . ."

"You love him, don't you?"

Susan nodded, tears falling afresh. "Pa said, 'No' when Wyatt asked his blessing," she continued in a moment. "He said no cowhand would ever marry his daughter. Wyatt was awful mad. He comes from a good family. Banjo can tell you that. They don't have much, like the Harringtons do." A bitter expression marred her pretty features for an instant. "Wyatt said he would have killed Pa if it wasn't for me."

"What?" Megan stared at Susan, instantly alert.

"He said he would have killed him," Susan repeated, defiantly. She stared at the low embers in the fireplace. "That's what's got me so upset, Megan. Wyatt was at the party, and he's good with a knife. I've seen him."

"You think he did it?" Megan could scarcely believe what she heard.

"I don't know," she said in a small, tortured voice. "I don't know." She fell silent, staring at the floor, still absently snarling her handkerchief.

"Let me get you a cup of tea."

Susan had regained some composure when Megan returned.

"I'm not accusing Wyatt," Susan said after taking a sip. "I don't know what to think."

"I can understand that."

"Things have been awful since Pa's funeral. I don't know how I can bear to stay there much longer. Beau is more arrogant than ever, bullying me, trying his best to irritate me. And that Clyde Turner, the foreman. He doesn't seem to know his place anymore. I heard him talking to Beau last night, and it sounded like he was giving orders, not taking them." She shivered.

"Then yesterday the marshal. . .what's his name? Oh, yes, Walker. . .came to the ranch. He was there all morning looking around and talking to the men. He spent a long time talking to Wyatt before he left. It scared me something fierce."

"Have you talked to Wyatt?"

"No, I've been afraid to. I guess I'm being foolish, but I can't help it." Susan set her teacup on the small table beside her chair.

"Why don't you lie down in my room for a while?" Megan suggested. "You're all in. A quiet rest would do you a world of good."

"I ought to be getting back," Susan protested weakly.

"For what? There's nothing for you to do there except mope. Come along." She took Susan's arm. "Steve probably won't be home until shortly before dark, so everything will be quiet."

"I guess you're right." She allowed Megan to lead her to the wide, quilt-covered bed.

"If you need anything, call out. I'm going to finish the ironing in the kitchen." Megan let down the curtain from its tie, dimming the room, and quietly went out.

Lifting the hot iron from its resting place on the stove, she thought about what Susan had told her. That Wyatt would murder the father of the woman he loved was inconceivable to Megan. If Wyatt killed Susan's father, Susan would turn against him, and he would lose the very thing he wanted.

Unless he lost his reason in a fit of rage.

She considered the possibility and rejected it. Maybe at the time Victor Harrington had humiliated him, but not months later. The problem weighed heavily on her mind long after Susan' had returned home.

≈

"I think a few strays have wandered out of the canyon," Banjo said when they sat around the fireplace after dinner that evening. "I saw some tracks leading toward Hohner's piece. I'd estimate there are probably less than ten cows, but I think it bears lookin' into. I didn't have time to do it today."

"Want to ride over that way tomorrow?" Steve looked up at Banjo from where he sat on the hearth plaiting a horsehair hackamore.

"Sure thing. It shouldn't take more'n half a day."

"Can I ride with you?" Megan asked impulsively. "It's been ages since I've been riding, and I'd like to get away from the house for a while."

"I guess it wouldn't hurt anything." Steve looked back down at his plaiting. "We'll leave at sunup."

Megan tingled with anticipation as she donned her riding habit the next morning. She could already feel the crisp autumn air and smell the pines. After all the heavy work of harvest time and the anxiety over the Harrington murder, she was ready for a change. She had been digging up vegetables, picking vegetables, canning vegetables, and jerking beef. She wanted to stretch her muscles, shake off the doldrums, and enjoy the day.

She packed a small tin with lunch, tied on her bonnet, and set off for the stable, Lobo close behind her. Whenever she stepped outdoors, he was always nearby.

Ears forward, head bobbing high, Candy was as eager to set off as Megan was. The strawberry roan nickered and nosed over Megan's clothes in search of a treat while Megan slid her Henry rifle into the saddle scabbard. She put her lunch tin in the saddlebag as she stood beside the mare to scratch under her mane before mounting up.

"Here's what you're looking for." Megan held out her palm, exposing a tiny mound of brown sugar. "You're a big baby," she said, patting Candy's nose affectionately. She stepped into the saddle with ease, enjoying the feel of the horse's movements beneath her, listening for the creak of leather.

"All set?" Steve called from the yard.

"Let's go!" Megan smiled happily, and lightly squeezed her knees on the mare's sides. When she reached Steve they set off together at an easy canter around the meadow with Banjo close behind.

They were halfway around when a rider came through the trees and trotted toward them. In the dim light of dawn it didn't take long to recognize Beau Harrington. He was alone.

"You still here, Chamberlin?" Beau shouted, menacingly. He drew his pinto horse to a halt near Steve. "I thought you'd have tucked your tail between your legs and run by now."

"Innocent men don't run," Steve said mildly, his hand resting on his thigh near his pistol. "What's your business, Harrington?"

"Thought I'd give you some friendly advice." He stared at Steve, hatred burning in his eyes. "The tin star had to go back to Denver. Seems he couldn't stay long enough to hang you. But don't you worry, the Rocking H can handle that job. You hang around asking for trouble, and we'll take care of you."

"That's the difference between you and me, Beau," Steve said. There was deadly stillness in his voice. "I don't ask for trouble. You came here looking for a fight. I'd hate to disappoint you."

Steve's hand shot out and grabbed Beau's shirt at the neck. He kicked the smaller man's boot from the stirrup and pushed him to the ground, falling on top of him. Caught off guard, Beau clutched frantically at the ironlike fist holding him.

Steve sat down across the smaller man's middle, drew back his free hand, and slapped Beau's freckled cheeks, back and forth again and again. Beau's red hair, now hatless, rolled in the dirt. A crimson drop oozed from the corner of his mouth.

Breathing heavily, Steve pulled young Harrington to his feet and backed away from him.

"You'd best get back where you belong before I decide to fight you like a man."

Beau's bruised lips drew back into a snarl of rage. Livid streaks adorned both cheeks. He clawed for his gun.

Beside Megan's horse, Lobo growled deep in his chest.

"I wouldn't do that if I were you, Harrington," Banjo said in a conversational voice.

Megan turned around to see the big buffalo gun lying in the old man's hands like it had been carved to fit.

"This here's a Sharps .56. It takes soft nose bullets. It ain't purty what they'll do to a man."

Harrington stiffened and slowly turned his eyes toward Banjo. At the sight of that wide, black bore pointed at him, he raised his hands. Slowly, keeping his hands wide, he reached down and picked up his hat, set it on his head, and scrambled for his horse. He missed the stirrup on the first try then mounted up. He jerked his horse around.

"We ain't done, Chamberlin!" he screeched. His face was the color of raw beefsteak. He gouged his spurs into the pinto's sides and galloped away.

When he had gone, Megan was shocked when she looked down to find that her rifle was in her hands, cocked and ready. She couldn't remember pulling it from the scabbard. She turned it wonderingly in her hands as though seeing it for the first time. Would she have used it? Her hands started shaking. The ague traveled up her arms until her shoulders were trembling. She slid the Henry rifle back into the scabbard and clenched her hands on the pommel. Sensing the change in Megan's attitude, Candy side-stepped a little.

"Are you all right?" Steve moved his mount close beside her. "Do you want to stay at the house?"

"No. I'll be okay." She moistened her lips, fighting for control. "I don't want to stay behind. Especially now. I'd spend the whole day doing nothing but worrying."

"If you say so," Steve said uncertainly. "If you feel too tired let me know, and we'll turn back."

"I'll be okay," she repeated as much to convince herself as to assure him. She gathered the reins tighter and straightened in the saddle. Steve gave her another searching look before leading out. Megan stayed beside him.

When they entered the woods, Megan fell behind Steve at the narrow spots, Banjo bringing up the rear. She studied her husband, with new eyes. He could have drawn a gun on Beau Harrington and killed him. It would have been called a fair fight. She knew Steve had the coolness that comes with maturity. Beau was hot-headed, too rash. He would have probably spoiled his first shot and been easy pickings for Steve. But Steve hadn't taken advantage of the younger man's temper in spite of the trouble Beau had caused him. An icy hand squeezed Megan's heart. She knew Beau would be back for revenge.

"Would you really have shot Beau this morning?" she asked Banjo later as they rode together on the trail. "I thought Christians were supposed to be peaceful."

"Christians shouldn't hunt trouble," Banjo replied, "but the Bible teaches that folks are supposed to obey the law. There's no lawman here to make sure that they do, so it's up to us law-abidin' folks to see the law is kept. Otherwise, the outlaws would soon run the rest of us off." His mild, blue eyes had that fatherly look again. "This is still a wild land, Miss Megan. When a peace officer comes to these parts, it'll be our Christian duty to let him do the keepin' of the law. Until then, we'll have to see to it."

"It scares me to think of what Beau will do next."

"Don't fret yourself," Banjo said. "Steve handled the situation this morning. He can handle it again." He drifted behind her. "Rock of Ages," he sang softly, and Megan urged Candy forward.

With Lobo still on their trail, they picked their way across rocky slopes and skirted huge boulders. Though it was only midafternoon, Megan's dress felt like it was pasted to her back. Her forehead and neck were clammy. When they reached the canyon where their cattle were pastured, Banjo moved around her and Steve to take the lead. Megan kept her eyes on Banjo when he leaned over Kelsey's gray shoulder to study the ground. Fifteen minutes of searching and he found the trail.

fourteen

The trail was easy to follow, and they moved along at a steady gait. They rode north over sagebrush-flecked hills, in and out of spruce and piñon pine, talking rarely, for almost an hour. The sky, full of great, billowing clouds when they left the house, had darkened to a muddy purple.

When they reached a large rock-strewn clearing, Banjo pulled up and dismounted. He knelt down, examining something in the dirt. In a moment Steve bent beside him. Megan came near enough to hear but kept her mount.

"The tracks join some others," Banjo remarked. "It appears some other cattle were drove through here sometime yesterday."

"Other cattle?" Steve asked.

"Not ours. They're coming from the wrong direction." He continued scouting around, his eyes examining every mound of dirt, every chipped stone.

"Well, looky here," he said at last.

Megan walked her horse closer and stepped down. Her curiosity grew by the minute. She looked over Banjo's shoulder. Lobo sniffed all around the tracks.

"See these horseshoes?" he said, softly. "They have an X carved into them." Megan could see the print plainly. "That's the mark Logan Hohner puts on his own shoes."

"Logan Hohner? Whose range is this?"

"We're heading into a corner where the Circle C, the Rocking H, and Hohner's outfit meet up. I think we're at the edge of Harrington's range. If not, we're close to it.

"It wouldn't have been Hohner himself that came through

115

here. He's always at the blacksmith shop in town. Must have been his boys." Banjo stood and knocked his hat to the back of his head. "I wonder what they was doin'."

A few drops of rain hit Megan's hand, and she looked toward the gray, swirling sky. Another drop hit her chin and another her cheek.

"There's a hollowed out spot in that boulder yonder." Banjo pointed to a rock face twenty feet high with a large stand of brush in front of it. "I've camped there a time or two."

Megan was surprised to see that behind the brush was an indentation in the rock about six feet by eight feet. They hadn't reached shelter any too soon. In seconds the rain was coming down like a heavy wind-blown curtain of water. From time to time a heavy gust blew some spray into the shelter.

Megan stood near the front watching the rain. Steve and Banjo moved inside to look around.

The remains of many campfires lay on one side with a little dry wood stacked not far away.

"Look at this." Steve picked up something from the ground.

"What is it?" Banjo asked.

"It's a twig." He held it out between thumb and finger for Banjo to see. "See how the bark is stripped halfway off, and one end has been chewed? It's not that old, either." He peeled a small piece of bark off. "See how much lighter the wood is under the bark? It hasn't completely dried out yet."

"Let me see that." Banjo stretched out his hand. "It looks mighty like the one I found at the Running M." He sniffed it. "It's juniper, too. It has a strong, sweet smell. It's a twin to the one I found after Harrington's murder."

"That's what I was thinking."

"Can I see it?" Megan asked, excitedly.

"Here." Banjo lightly tossed it to her. "Put it someplace safe." He turned back to the area he had been studying. "Let's look close. We may have hit pay dirt."

"This fire is only a day or two old," Banjo said, kneeling

beside it. "Some of the coals are smooth, and some are jagged. The jagged coals are new."

"Let's quarter the area," Steve suggested. "I'll take the right side, Banjo." He held up a warning hand. "Don't come too close, Megan. You may ruin some good sign without knowing it. Stay where you are until we have a chance to look the place over real carefullike."

Leaning her shoulder against the rock, Megan fell into watchful silence. Lobo finally came in out of the rain. He sat by Megan's skirt, and she absently put her hand on his ruff. His fur was wet and foul. Disgusted, she looked at her grimy hand. It had a repulsive, wet doggy smell. She scrubbed at it with her handkerchief and made herself (and Lobo) an unspoken promise.

"Well, what do you know?" Banjo said in a half-whisper a few minutes later. "Here's a boot print. A clear one, not scuffed out like the rest. It looks like the ground was soft when he stepped here and it dried without being disturbed." He knelt on one knee. "Old boots, I'd say. Run-down at the heel. And a big man. Two hundred pounds at least."

"Any idea who it may be?" Steve asked.

"There's quite a few big men hereabouts." Banjo shook his head. "I wouldn't want to venture a guess. You got anything else?"

"No, can't say I do." Steve carefully searched the ground at his feet.

Megan placed the twig in the pocket of her riding habit. She resolved again to watch for a man who chewed twigs. Many men she had seen chewed straws. She couldn't remember anyone chewing a twig.

The rain had let up a little when Megan's stomach reminded her it was lunch time.

"I'm hungry." Megan's voice sounded small. The men turned quickly. They had almost forgotten she was along.

"Let's eat." Steve walked toward her. "I could use a bite myself." He ran through the rain to retrieve the lunch tin from Megan's saddlebag.

"That Harrington boy won't soon forget the whoppin' you gave him this morning," Banjo said, helping himself to a second piece of corn bread.

Megan, already finished, idly twirled a yellow cottonwood leaf with brown edges, holding the stem between her thumb and forefinger. She glanced at Steve who was wiping his mouth with the back of his hand, and waited tensely for his answer.

"I know it." He took a sip from his canteen. "He's a bully, but I don't want to kill him if I can help it, Banjo."

"I respect you for it, Chamberlin, but you'll have to be on your guard. I wouldn't put it past the young pup to burn the house around your ears if he happened to think of it."

The old panicky feeling came back to Megan in full force. "What are you going to do?" she asked Steve. "Even Susan's afraid of Beau. He may do something terrible."

"You don't have to be afraid of the house burning. The sides and back are wood, but they're solid logs." Steve lay back on the grass, an arm under his head. "It would take a mighty big match to get them going. Now the stable would be a different story altogether."

"Maybe Banjo should start sleeping in the house—" Megan stopped in midsentence. She suddenly realized what that would mean to her and Steve's arrangement. She bowed her head, pretending to examine the leaf in her hand to hide the redness she could feel warming her cheeks.

"No, Miss Megan," Banjo said. "I need to stay in the stable to keep watch. Who will warn you otherwise?"

"If we do have trouble at night," Steve added, "come to the house through the back door. Just bust in and get us up."

"I'll surely do that." Banjo rose stiffly to his feet. "That was good, Miss Megan. I sure am glad I don't have to live with my own cookin' anymore. And there's always plenty. I appreciate that, too. There was times when I was so poor and hungry I had to cut my corn bread in half so I could get enough to eat."

"Cut it in half?"

"Yeah, so I could have two pieces instead of one." Chuckling, he peered outside. "Rain's stopped. We may as well move on."

Shaking her head, Megan smiled at the joke. She picked up the lunch tin and followed the men.

The shower had wiped away the tracks, but Steve led out in the direction they had been following before the storm. Ten minutes later they came on six young Circle C cows bunched together by a stream. It was short work to drive them back to the herd.

෨

No one came to the clearing during the next week, not even Susan. The last of the canning was finished. The turnips were covered with straw so they wouldn't freeze in the ground and could be dug during the winter. Megan looked over her full cupboards with a deep sigh of satisfaction. The work had been hard, but now she was thankful.

She was pinning a last pair of jeans to the clothesline beside the house when she caught sight of Lobo lying on his back, legs spread-eagle, napping in the sun. Lobo was basking in the warmth, because the nights were windy and cold. The warm sunshine chased the gripping chill from his doggy bones. The smell of wood smoke from the fireplace and Banjo's potbelly stove in the stable made the air smell as well as feel like autumn.

Clothes basket in hand, Megan marveled at the change in the wolf-faced dog. His hipbones were no longer easy to see. He was quick to wag his tail and give short, happy barks when she played with him. He had lost his fear of Steve and Banjo, but barked ferociously when a stranger rode in.

She set the laundry basket in the kitchen and went out by the spring to dump out the dirty wash water. She wished Jeremy could see Lobo. They would love each other. The warm, soapy water sloshed as she raised the edge of the tub. She was about to give the final heave, but suddenly stopped.

Eyes on the few remaining soapsuds, she thought some more about Lobo.

"Lobo, my boy," she said aloud to herself, "today is a red

letter day for you."

She opened the back door of the stable and called the unsuspecting dog. Tail wagging, tongue lolling, he trotted into the stable. He licked her hand once before sniffing her skirt, the ground, the doorway.

"Come on, boy." She led the way through the door with Lobo close behind. "I know you think I have something for you to eat. . .get down! I don't want your dirty paws on my skirt." She looked at the spot. "Oh, well, I guess it doesn't matter. Who knows what I'll look like by the time this project is over."

She led him to the edge of the tub. How to go about getting him into the tub was the next problem, after that how to keep him there. She put her forearms under his middle near his front and back legs. He licked her face and uncertainly waved his thick tail. Megan gasped when she hoisted him into the water.

"You certainly have put on weight," she panted, her hands holding him firmly. There was marked doubt in Lobo's eyes now. He sniffed the surface of the water and looked longingly at the stable door he had just come through.

"Be still, Lobo," Megan said, soothingly. "It'll all be over in a minute. Make that five or ten minutes. I promise to hurry." She picked up the bar of soap and rubbed it over his back.

The transformation took fifteen minutes. In that short space of time Lobo's gray, matted fur turned ivory, the brown was rust-colored, the black dark gray instead of soot. Megan, on the other hand, changed from a neat, albeit slightly damp, house-wife to a dirt-smudged, gray-flecked, dog-smelling woman. When she set Lobo free, he gave his shaggy coat a healthy shake to further adorn his mistress.

"What happened to Lobo?" Steve asked her that afternoon on their way to shoot targets. "He have a fight with a scrubbing brush?"

"You could say that," Megan laughed. "I stuck him in my wash tub after I finished the clothes." She looked lovingly at the fluffy animal at her side. It was hard to see a wolf resemblance now.

She reached down to scratch behind a pointed ear.

"Do you want to go with me to Juniper tomorrow?"

"That would be nice," Megan answered, happily. "I have a letter to mail. I hope there will be one waiting for me, too." She broke open her rifle to check the load and then snapped it shut. "What are we shooting today?"

Her hopes were fulfilled the next morning when the young postmaster handed her a small, white envelope. She tore it open and scanned the contents. When she finished, the hand holding the letter fell limply to her side. She stepped outside and stood motionless on the boardwalk with the letter still crumpled in her hand. Jeremy had taken a turn for the worse. He was weak. The doctor was anxious.

Sheer willpower forced the tears back. Where could she hide to have a good cry?

"Megan!" Susan's voice startled her.

"Oh, hello." Megan shoved the letter into her skirt pocket.

"Bad news?" Susan asked, looking at her friend's strained face.

"Not really bad, just disappointing," Megan managed. "How are you?" She steered the conversation away from herself. If she had to talk about Jeremy now she would burst into tears.

"Not too good." Susan stepped close to the wall of the postal station, away from easy view. "I saw what Steve did to Beau's face." She held up a hand against Megan's reply. "I'm glad, Megan. He needed someone to bring him down a notch. He wouldn't show himself outside the ranch until yesterday. I got him to bring me into town today." She glanced up the street. "I can't let him see me talking to you.

"Be careful." Susan was in dead earnest. "Beau says he's going to settle accounts with Steve, and he doesn't have any scruples. Tell your husband."

"Thank you, Susan." Megan clasped Susan's hand.

Tears shone brightly in Susan's eyes. She gave Megan's hand an answering squeeze and hurried away.

The letter in Megan's pocket had drained all the pleasure out of the outing. She was all in before Steve was ready to leave. The buckboard was parked in the shade of Harper's Emporium so she put her few packages into the back and climbed heavily to the seat. Sitting in the shadow was much better than plaguing her shoe-pinched feet any longer. She lay her hand on her skirt and felt the paper crackle.

Poor little Jeremy. If only he could come to Colorado and play in the clear sunshine. She pictured him running free and strong in the meadow romping with Lobo. Another crackle of the letter in her pocket and the picture shattered, leaving a painful emptiness in the pit of her stomach.

Did I make the right decision? In trying to give him more than I could afford, did I take away what he needed most: love, security. . .myself?

"Bad news?" Steve asked when he joined her.

"Jeremy is worse." She tried to say it without betraying her agitation, but her voice cracked. She pressed her arms against her sides and smoothed her skirt with small movements.

"Is there anything I can do for him? Does he have the best doctors?"

"The best the sanitarium has to offer, I guess."

"Let me get him the best one in Baltimore."

"Do you know how much that would cost?"

"I know. But it doesn't matter. I'll go to the telegraph office and send Tump my instructions."

"I appreciate what you're trying to do, but the doctor alone will take up more than all my wages."

"Consider it a gift. No strings attached." He jumped to the ground. "No more arguments," he said, firmly. "It's settled."

She was relieved Jeremy would be getting better care, yet she wasn't sure how to take Steve's offer. Or his insistence. Why was he doing this? In all their struggles against poverty, her mother had never taken charity. She didn't want charity, either. Was that what Steve's gift was?

A flash of sunlight on silver caught her eye. It came from

Clyde Turner, the Rocking H foreman, who was standing in front of the Red Rooster Saloon. He was wearing black pants with silver studs down the sides. On his black boots were huge silver spurs. The pants were topped by a silky black shirt with a gray kerchief. Fascinated, Megan watched him. She had never seen a cowhand turned out like that before.

Arms folded, Turner loafed against the hitching rail. He kept looking down the street like he was waiting for someone. Henry and Al Hohner shambled down the dusty street and walked up to talk to him. Glancing around secretively, he spoke a few words to them and strode into the saloon, causing the doors to swing to and fro several times after he passed. Al and Henry continued down the street in the direction of their father's shop.

"All set." Steve was at her side before she saw him. "I left instructions that we are to be wired of his condition within the week."

Megan drew a deep breath. There was nothing more to say.

Scraping the hoof of a horse, Logan Hohner stood outside his blacksmith's shop on the edge of town. He straightened and waved for them to stop when the buckboard drew near. Steve pulled up, and Hohner shuffled over to them.

"Gud afternoon, Mr. Chamberlin. Ma'am." The gap in his teeth was conspicuous when he smiled. His jaw was coarse with a thick patch of stubble. "I vanted to tell ye that I doan mind de gossips und all de slander dey be speakin' about ye. Ye can come to me any time to have work done." He leaned forward, speaking in a loud whisper. "Dey lie about my boys, too. My boys is gud boys. Dey never did no rustlin' in dere lifes." He leaned back and stuck his thumbs under his over-stretched suspenders. "So you cum to Logan Hohner if ye need someding."

Megan absently watched the Rocking H hands ride out of town.

"Thank you, Mr. Hohner. I'll be sure to do that." Steve clucked to the horses and the buckboard jostled ahead.

When they were on the trail out of town, Steve cleared his throat. "I had an interesting conversation while we were in town. I saw Jim Sanders outside the Emporium shortly before you came. As

Banjo would say, he was as jumpy as a June bug at a poultry convention. He said not to worry, the gossip about Harrington's murder would die down before long. He thought Harrington deserved what he got. Whoever did it did a service to the community, so to speak. Then he left at almost a dead run." He shrugged. "I can't figure out why he was telling me all that."

"I saw something interesting, too." She told him about the incident between Clyde Turner and the Hohner boys.

"Most cowhands couldn't afford that getup," Steve agreed.

"He's the foreman, though," Megan reasoned. "And the Harringtons probably pay a pretty good wage."

"That Turner definitely reminds me of someone," Steve said. "The more I see of him, the more it strikes me. But for the life of me I can't put a name to him."

Suddenly, a shot shattered the afternoon stillness. The four horses pulling the buckboard instantly bolted. They charged down the rough trail as though driven by an insane wagon master. Bracing her feet against the front of the wagon, Megan gripped the seat, her knuckles white, trying to stay aboard.

"Whoa!" Steve shouted frantically. "Whoa!" Raising the reins high, he leaned back on the lines with all his might, but still the horses ran. The rushing wind caught Steve's hat, sending it sailing. The plain was a brown blur. On and on the buckboard flew, bouncing, swaying, careening down the trail.

Frothing at the mouth, eyes wild, the horses bounded on. Megan's arms ached from clinging to the seat. She knew she couldn't hold on much longer.

The front wheel on her side slid into a small gully, and she felt the wagon tilt. Scrambling, clawing for a hold, she heard the splinter of cracking wood and the terrified scream of a horse. The buckboard fell heavily on its side, throwing her to the stony ground. She had the sensation of falling, felt a stabbing pain in her right shoulder, and everything went black.

fifteen

"Megan? Megan?" A gentle hand touched her face. She raised her arm to touch the hand. The movement brought another stabbing pain to her shoulder, and she moaned.

"Megan?" It was Steve.

She opened her eyes to see him kneeling beside her, bending close to her face.

"My shoulder hurts when I move it."

"Don't try to move until I check it out." He rubbed gentle fingers over her upper arm and shoulder. "Tell me when it hurts."

"Now." She winced.

"Move your fingers. Okay, now your lower arm."

She had to force herself to obey, clenching her teeth against the pain.

"I don't think it's broken, but it may be out of joint. I'm taking you back to the doctor in Juniper."

She looked at his scraped, dirt-covered face so full of concern for her.

"You're hurt yourself," she breathed.

"Just a few scrapes." His jaw grew hard. "I wish I had the scoundrel who did this!"

"What?" His words frightened her.

"Someone burned Caesar's back with a bullet. That's what set the horses to running. You could have been killed."

He ran his hand through his wind-blown hair. "I've been a fool, Megan, thinking I could win against that Harrington outfit. We're bucking a stacked deck. I had no right to bring a woman out here in the first place." His eyes were windows to a tormented soul. "I think we ought to catch the next train back to Baltimore."

"But—" She tried to sit up, but the ache in her shoulder made her lie back. "We can't! Do you know what you're saying?"

"I can't stand to have them hurt you. Why can't they face me and fight like a man?" He slammed an iron fist into his callused palm.

Dr. Leatherwood, the new doctor in Juniper Junction, told them the shoulder was only badly sprained. He bound it up and put her right arm in a sling.

"Wrap the shoulder in brown paper soaked in vinegar twice a day," he instructed as Megan prepared to go. "Leave it on for half an hour and then replace this binding." He was a young man, probably not much older than Steve. He was prematurely bald and his nose looked like it had been broken more than once. In fact he looked more like a boxer than a doctor.

"You'll have to rest the arm for at least a week. Ten days if it still pains you." He handed Steve a small, brown envelope when they came out of the examination room. "Give her a little of this if she can't rest because of pain. And feel free to call on me again if you have any problems."

"Thank you, Doctor." Steve gave Megan a relieved smile and opened the door for her.

"You've already got it fixed." Megan looked at the front rigging of the buckboard where it had cracked.

"I took it over to the blacksmith while the doc was looking at you. He did a smart job."

"I'll say." She supported the sling with her left hand. "I wasn't looking forward to limping home like we did to get back to town." Her arm ached frightfully from her elbow to her shoulder and neck.

"You think you ought to lie down in the back?" He looked anxiously at her wan expression.

"I think the jarring of the wagon would be worse that way than if I sat up."

"I'll try to take it easy on the ruts."

"Just get us there as fast as you can," Megan said through tense lips.

It was an endless, grueling journey. Every jostle was an irritation, every jolt an agony. Darkness fell before they had reached the stand of pines and oaks around the meadow. The pain was nauseating. White to the lips, she clamped her arm against her middle to keep it still.

"Why don't you lean against me?" Steve asked, sliding close to her.

Weakly, Megan lay her head against his shoulder and closed her eyes. The change of position did ease her arm some. She was weary beyond endurance.

"You were right back there when I was spouting off. I don't want to leave the ranch," he said at length. "It's more than my father's inheritance. I've come to love the place."

"I know," Megan said, softly. "It's so good to have open spaces and fresh air after living in the city. If it weren't for Jeremy, I wouldn't ever want to go back."

"You know what I said about putting down roots here?"

"Yes," she said, wincing as the buckboard bounced into a dry puddle.

"I want do to that. Stay here and work the land, raise some beef. . . ." His voice drifted off, and they rode in silence the rest of the way home.

"Megan's been hurt," Steve told Banjo when they arrived at the stone house. "Ride over to the Rocking H and see if you can talk to Susan without anyone knowing. I don't want to cause her more trouble. Just tell her Megan could use her help for a few days."

Ignoring her feeble protests, Steve carried Megan to the house and lay her on the bed. Tears of pain and exhaustion trickled down the sides of her face toward her ears.

"Here, take this powder. It'll help you sleep." He handed her a full spoon of powder stirred into a glass of water.

Raising her head off the pillow she swallowed the medicine and shivered at the bitter taste. Steve took the glass from her hand.

"Thank you for looking after me," she said, weakly.

"Don't talk." He turned down the lamp beside her bed until it was a dull glow. "I'll check in on you in a while."

The lamp was still glowing dimly when she awakened. A

blanket covered her to the chin. She touched it, wondering how it got there. Sleepily pulling it aside, she sat up. She was thirsty. Thinking of the pitcher of water in the kitchen, she put her toes on the cold floor and realized for the first time that her shoes had been removed. She must have been sleeping like the dead to have stayed asleep when they were taken off.

Her shoulder still ached, but not as sharply as before. Moving slowly through the gloomy room, she reached the open door of her room and paused. In the fireplace hot coals glowed brilliant orange, casting an eerie light over the room. When her eyes adjusted she recognized Steve's figure rolled in a blanket on the floor in front of the hearth. His back was toward her, but she could tell from his position that he was asleep.

Putting her hand out before her like a blind person, she started across the room. She had taken only three steps when Steve rolled over and came to his feet in one move.

"What are you doing up?" He blinked and peered at her through sleep-dulled eyes. "You should have called me."

"I wanted a drink." She felt like a schoolgirl caught passing a note.

"Go back and lie down. I'll fetch it for you."

"Banjo left a message for Susan with Wyatt," he said as he gave her a glass of cold spring water. "Hopefully she'll be here in the morning."

Megan drank long and deep. The cold water felt good on her parched throat.

"You shouldn't take on about me so." She handed him the empty glass. "I'll be all right. There's nothing terribly wrong with my arm. It won't hurt me to move around some."

"Tomorrow you'll be sore in places you didn't even know you had. Take it from one who knows. You'll be glad I sent for Susan." He pulled the cover over her. "You need any more of that powder to get back to sleep?"

"I don't think so." She yawned.

"Well, if you need anything else give a holler. I'll be right outside."

&

The gray light of morning made a segmented square on the wall of her room. Half-asleep, she tried to roll over and she felt a stab in her shoulder. The accident came back to her in the same instant. The creak of the opening front door had awakened her.

"How is she?" It was Susan's voice.

Steve replied, "She's sleeping. Seemed to rest fairly well through the night."

"What happened?"

Megan heard Susan's light steps cross the stone floor, and Steve told the story in five sentences. Susan, dressed in her black silk mourning clothes, was standing in the bedroom doorway moments later.

"Good morning." Megan tried to sound cheerful.

"I'm so sorry." Susan came to the bed and bent over her. "Does it hurt much?" She looked anxiously at the sling.

"Not so much now. It's a dull ache." She shifted her position on the bed. "Steve was right. I do ache all over this morning."

"You relax." Susan pulled off her black gloves. "I'll have you a nice, hot breakfast in no time." She was tugging at her bonnet strings as she went out.

"I've got some things to attend to on the range." Steve stepped into her room when Susan was gone. "I'll be back at supper time." He came a step closer. "You be good and stay quiet."

"The way I feel I can't do anything else." She tried to say it flippantly, but the words fell a little flat. Steve's expression unnerved her so much she couldn't think of anything else to say.

His face was full of compassion, but behind his eyes was something alive. He picked up her hand and held it between both of his. He didn't speak anymore, either, just stood there looking down at her. Megan felt strength in his gentle touch. She sensed fire beneath his tender concern. It gave her a sweet, warm feeling, but frightened her a little, too.

He replaced her hand on the quilt like a collector setting down a rare piece of crystalware; he took a step backward and went out.

She wanted to analyze his expression, relive the sensation of his hand holding hers, but it was too tiring. She nestled her head deeper into the pillow.

Brilliant light cascaded over the bed when Susan tied up the curtain. Megan squinted against the glare. She must have fallen asleep.

"I've brought you some hot biscuits and tea," Susan said, placing a tray over her knees.

"Thanks." Megan slowly and painfully eased up into a sitting position and adjusted the sling around her neck. "I don't know what I would have done if you hadn't come over."

Susan's smile matched the sunbeams spilling through the window. "Wyatt woke me up last night. He threw pebbles at my window. It was very romantic."

"Really?" Megan came to life. "Did he say anything else besides Banjo's message?"

"That would be tellin'." Susan laughed lightly and Megan noticed that though it was September, for Susan roses were back in season. "He said he'd come over here if he got a chance."

"What did you tell your brother? About coming over, I mean." Megan took a small bite of a buttered biscuit.

"I left a note saying that a friend of mine wasn't feeling well, and I'd be away helping her for a few days. What he doesn't know won't hurt him in this case."

"I hope you don't have any trouble because of me." The worried look returned to Megan's face.

"Never mind." Susan took the tray from Megan's lap. "Rest. You'll never get better if you lie there and fret. I'll have your brown paper and vinegar in a few minutes."

The stench of the vinegar was stifling but it did seem to help the pain as it soaked into her sore muscles. Slowly, Megan moved her lower arm up and down.

"It's a miracle it wasn't broken!" Susan exclaimed when she saw the dark blue bruise on Megan's shoulder and upper arm.

"I've never seen a runaway horse before." Megan shuddered. "And when the wagon started tipping. . . ."

"Don't dwell on it," Susan interrupted. "Let's get the dressing back on now and you can have a rest.

"Would you like me to read to you or do you want to sleep?" she asked when Megan was lying down again.

"I'll sleep. I'm worn out. I can't believe how something so small can make me feel so tired."

Sometime later, the sound of the front door opening awakened Megan for the second time that day.

"Susan." It was a young man's deep voice.

"Hello, Wyatt."

"How's Mrs. Chamberlin?"

"She's resting." Light footsteps sounded on the stone floor. "Would you like to sit down?"

"I need to talk to you, Susan," he said, urgently. "Things are bad with you and Beau, aren't they?" Pause. "You don't have to tell me. I know they are. Why don't you come away with me? We can go to Montana or Oregon and start a life for ourselves. There's nothing left for us here."

"I wish I could, Wyatt, but it's impossible." There was a frustrated longing in her words.

"What's the holdup?" he demanded impatiently. "There's nothing to stand between us now."

"I can't leave Colorado without knowing who killed Pa. After the murderer is caught and punished I may consider it, but right now it's out of the question." She hesitated, then plunged on. "I've got to ask you something. Please don't be angry with me. I think I already know the answer, but I have to hear you say it."

"What is it?"

"Did you do it?"

"Kill your pa? Of course not!"

"I didn't think you did, Wyatt. I had to hear you say it." She sounded on the verge of tears.

Megan sank deeper into her pillow and closed her eyes. She didn't like overhearing their conversation.

"He was a scoundrel," Wyatt went on, "and I have to admit I hated him, but I didn't kill him. I was tempted to the night he turned me down, but I knew you loved him. Not that I could understand why you did. I would never do such a lowdown thing to you as that."

"You don't know how relieved I am. I've wanted to talk to you a hundred times since the funeral, but I was too afraid of being overheard."

"To tell you the truth, I think a rustler killed your pa. While we were on the cattle drive, I heard him talking to his foreman and one of the hands. He said he thought one of the hands must be in on the rustling, because it's been going on so long. This was the fourth year the count was low. And this year it was the worst of all."

"Do you have any idea who it could be?"

"It's hard to tell. There's quite a few of the hands may have done some underhanded things in their time. A person don't ask about those things. You know that." He paused. "Things are getting pretty rough at the ranch. Some of the hands are talking about asking for their wages. If it weren't for you, Susan, I'd pull out, too."

"Don't. Please, don't leave me there all alone."

"I was sort of hoping you'd see it that way." His voice surged with a strong undercurrent. "You haven't given me much encouragement the last while. I was starting to fear you'd changed your mind about us."

"I could never change my mind, Wyatt." Susan spoke softly, intensely.

Boots scraped against the floor, and a chair creaked. Then silence.

"I can't stay too long. Turner'll miss me and ask me a lot of questions I don't want to answer. He sure has been on the prod lately. He's about as easy to work with as an irritated porcupine."

After a few minutes of silence the door opened and the clumping of heavy boots on the porch told Megan he was gone. Megan lay still, feigning sleep when Susan came in. She was happy for Susan, but even as she rejoiced, she wrestled another emotion: a strange, deep yearning. It was the sweet agony of discovering a deep, pure vein of gold at the bottom of a craggy cliff, a cliff so loosely seamed that one blow with a pick would bring the mountain crashing down on the miner's head.

It was the knowledge of something precious with no hope of having it for her own. She savored the new sensation, and tried to understand it.

sixteen

"How are you comin' on, Miss Megan?" Banjo asked the next evening. He and Steve sat by Megan's bed for a chat after supper while Susan finished the dishes.

"Restless." Megan sat propped against some pillows. Her arm was still too sore to move freely.

"I rode back to the place where the horses stampeded," Steve said, "but I couldn't find a clue."

"Who would do such a terrible thing?" Megan asked, cradling her sling in her strong arm.

"Someone who wants to get rid of you folks mighty bad," Banjo offered.

"Wyatt was here today," Megan said. "He thinks Harrington had an idea that one of his own hands had a part in the cattle rustling."

"The Rocking H hands are a hard bunch, but I've my doubts that any of them would be a thief," Banjo said, thoughtfully. "'Course, there are a couple new ones I don't know so good."

"Wyatt said they've had cattle missing for four years now," Megan continued. "It would have to be someone who has been with them longer than that."

"I'd have to study on it a while, I reckon." He shifted in his chair. "With your permission, Chamberlin, I'll ride over toward that corner of the range we were on a few days ago and have another look-see. I believe the man who stood under that shelter the night Harrington was killed is the same man who was in that cave."

"Shoo, you men," Susan scolded from the door. "Can't you see Megan's tired?"

"Susan's making herself right to home," Banjo said to Steve with an unusually serious expression. "Reminds me of a sergeant I knew in the Confederate army."

"Don't pay him any mind, Susan," Megan advised, smiling. "He's like a toothless lion, a big roar with nothing to back it up."

"Everybody around here knows Banjo," Susan countered, "and we make allowances for the aged and infirmed."

"All right." Banjo chuckled. "I know when I'm bested."

Later that night Steve came into her room, closed the door, and made up his bed on the floor where he'd been sleeping since Susan came. He paused, blanket in hand.

"Still hurt bad?" he asked, referring to her arm.

"Not as much as at first, but it's still sore. I expect Susan will be able to go home day after tomorrow."

"I don't think she's in any hurry." He spread out the blanket and sat on it. "I feel for her, living with that hot-headed brother of hers."

"So do I." Megan turned her face toward the wall and closed her eyes. She lay a long while half-asleep, missing Jeremy and Em, thinking of Susan and Wyatt, listening to Steve's deep, regular breathing as he slept on the floor at her feet.

❧

"I found it," Banjo announced the next day. The three of them sat around the table after Megan's first lunch outside her room. Susan had ridden home for some fresh clothing. "The purtiest little box canyon you ever did see."

"Where?" Steve asked.

"A little north of where we found the camp. It's Hohner's range. I'm sure of it. A hundred acres of nice grazing and a stream running through one end. Had maybe two hundred head of cattle. Good lookin', young stuff. I'd say they're all two years old or less.

"I scouted around and found another camp near the stream.

And get this," he leaned forward, "it had the same marked horse-shoe tracks and the same juniper twigs."

Steve whistled softly.

"Most of the cattle were too young to hold a brand, but I saw a couple steers with a doctored Circle R. The top half of the brand was new, hadn't healed proper yet. It's my guess they're Rocking H cattle."

"What are you going to do?" Megan asked.

"Sit tight," Steve answered. "We don't know who's doing it yet."

"But it must be Logan Hohner." Megan persisted.

"Not necessarily," Banjo said. "I think someone is using Hohner's land without him knowing it." He paused and shifted his toothpick to the other side of his mouth. "Knowing Logan Hohner, he hasn't seen that canyon for a couple o' years." He shook his head. "His boys are probably in on it in some way, but I think we need to look a little further before we can find the person behind it, the rottenness at the core."

"You think someone is putting Hohner's boys up to it?" Steve asked.

"That's about it. Those Hohner boys aren't smart enough for a long-term operation like this'n. Their boss has to make a slip-up sometime, and with us knowing what to look for, we should be able to catch him."

❧

In a few days, Megan's arm was in working order again. It was weak, and she had to rest often, but she was able to carry out her household chores.

The promised telegram from the new sanitarium made Megan cry from glad relief. Jeremy was responding to the more expensive treatment. The doctor was encouraged by his progress in the few days he had been there. She hugged the news to her like a woolly blanket on a cold, wintry night.

"The circuit riding preacher is coming through next Sunday,"

Banjo said, pausing after breakfast. "I wondered if you were feeling up to attending. I plan on going myself. A body don't get much chance to hear real preaching in these parts."

"I'd love to go," Megan said. "I'm sure Steve'll let us use the buckboard. Maybe he'll want to go himself. I'll ask him."

Steve shook his head doubtfully when she brought up the subject that evening.

"That's all right. You and Banjo take the buckboard and go," he replied. "I'll stay here and look after things."

She was disappointed by Steve's blunt refusal to join them, but the feeling was short-lived. She was too excited to let anything dampen her spirits. This would be the first church service she would attend as a Christian. She was looking forward to it even more than she had the frolic.

The buckboard rattled over the leaf-strewn trail on that fine, hope-filled Sunday morning. Only Billy and Star were hitched up today since they weren't going for supplies. It was a cool, crisp day. Megan pulled her white, knotted shawl closer around her pink dress with the starched white collar. She took a deep breath of the tingly breeze. Beside her, Banjo looked like a stranger in his carefully brushed black suit and black string tie. Without its usual growth of stubble, his face looked like a freshly skinned squirrel.

"Preacher Tyler is a young feller, but he can really preach." Banjo tugged at his celluloid collar. "He's been traveling through these parts for purty nigh three years. Don't have no real home. He keeps moving from place to place. Goes all the way from Montana to Texas, I hear." He glanced at Megan. "Don't expect no fancy sermonizing like that city feller from Denver who preached at Harrington's funeral. But you'll carry something home with you to hide in your heart against the hard places in life."

"Do many people come to the meetings?"

"Quite a few. Most of them because they go to every social

gathering that comes along. But there are a few real saints in Juniper. I'll be proud to introduce you to 'em."

"I'm looking forward to it, Banjo."

The schoolhouse was half-filled when they arrived. The desks had been removed and long, backless benches filled the room. They were crammed so closely together that Megan could barely get her skirts though the aisle. Banjo found seats for them near the center of the room. The seats near the windows were already taken, and the air felt stuffy. A hushed buzzing hovered over the group as folks chatted before the service. Megan recognized Mr. and Mrs. Harper coming in. They nodded, unsmiling, in her direction and found places on the far left. Elaine Sanders gave her a small, noncommittal wave from across the room where she chatted gaily with a blond young man Megan didn't know.

A steady stream of people poured in until the room was packed shoulder to shoulder, knee to back. Megan's light, cotton dress, so cool this morning, was becoming itchy with its high collar and long sleeves. Megan tried not to fidget, but she was impatient for the service to begin.

The sermon was simple and direct. In spite of the warmness of the room and the closeness of the congregation, Megan forgot all but the power of the message. The preacher's dark suit was shiny at the elbows and knees, and there was little to draw the eye to his rawboned, pock-scarred face. But Megan had never seen a man so completely absorbed in his message. She could tell he really believed what he preached.

"You must be born again," he urged, his voice quiet, intense, as he pleaded with the lost. And on he spoke, "Why call on the Lord and then not do the things He commands you to do?"

Megan's spirit was gripped. At the end of the message, she stood with others who wanted to surrender to God's will for their lives. Yet even as she stood, there was confusion and anxiety inside her soul. What of her marriage to Steve? What of her future?

She brushed her anxious thoughts aside to nod and smile in response to Banjo's introductions after the service. She especially liked Mrs. Stowe, a small middle-aged widow with wavy, chestnut brown hair and a motherly smile.

"Be sure to stop and have a cup of tea with me when you're in town," Mrs. Stowe urged. "I'd love to hear about Baltimore and the East. I'll pray for your brother, too," she promised when Megan told her about Jeremy.

Megan was touched by Mrs. Stowe's sincere kindness and promised to stop and visit the widow when she came to town.

The preacher's quick smile and friendly handshake were also encouraging.

"I'm glad to see you take your stand for Christ, Mrs. Chamberlin," he said. "I'll be sure to pray for you in the days to come. Satan would like to discourage you, but God is a strong tower. When you feel temptation, run to God and He'll keep you safe." He gave Banjo a friendly punch in the shoulder. "You can depend on Banjo to give you good advice if you need it. We go back a long way together. He prays for me. It's folks like him keep me on the circuit."

It was an hour past noon when they set off on the trail out of town. They had barely passed the last frame building when Banjo untied his string tie and pulled off his collar.

"Excuse me, Miss Megan, but I can't abide this contraption any longer. Puts me in mind of being tied with a rope halter." He stuffed the black string and bit of celluloid into his shirt pocket.

Megan picked up the basket of food she had packed for their lunch and handed Banjo a thick beef sandwich.

"Much obliged," he said, taking a bite.

Lost in thought, she finished her lunch and packed away the leftovers. What about her marriage to Steve? What of the future?

seventeen

"There's power in the blood, power in the blood. . . ." Banjo's song reached far across the brown, evergreen-spotted hills. When they started to climb the mountain trail, he stopped singing. "I don't want to be buttin' in where I don't belong, but it appears to me something's troublin' you, Miss Megan," he said. "I don't want to know your business, but you know I'd do anything I can to help."

"I know you would, Banjo," Megan replied, carefully. "I'm thinking of the decision I made this morning and wondering what the future holds for me." She looked at her hands, clasping and unclasping them in her lap.

"It's Chamberlin, ain't it?"

Megan pressed her lips together and nodded. "You see, we don't have the usual relationship." She turned her head away from him, gazing out over the bare trees and rocks. Feeling a chilly breeze, she tightened the shawl around her shoulders. "We're really married, and all, but we're not. . . ." She sighed. "It's hard to explain."

"I knowed it. I knowed it all along."

"You knew? How?"

"You told me yourself." He smiled at her doubtful expression. "Oh, not in so many words. But you didn't act like a young newly married couple. I'm no spring chick. I've been down the pike and across the river, you know. And one morning I came to the house early for breakfast and I saw him coming down from the loft. It didn't take much figuring to work it out."

"I met him only a few weeks before we came here. He had to have a wife to fulfill his father's will. We have to live on the

139

ranch for a year in order to collect his inheritance. He actually hired me to do it." She pressed her lower lip between her teeth, unable to go on.

"You did it for Jeremy, didn't you?"

Looking down at her restless hands, she nodded.

"He had to go to a sanitarium, and I didn't have the money. It is legal. The marriage, I mean. We didn't cheat on that."

"So what's got you so wrought up? You and Chamberlin seem to hit it off all right."

"Next May he's going to have the marriage dissolved, and I'll go back to Baltimore. I g-guess it shouldn't matter to me." She dabbed at the tears, blinking others back. "Jeremy is getting better, the doctor said. It's just that when I think of having to leave someday, I get all scared inside. I don't know what will happen to me."

"You're in love with him, aren't you?"

Megan stared at him. She wanted to cry out, "No, I'm not!" but her lips were silent. Was she in love with Steve? She couldn't say no. If she had said the words they would have been a lie.

Like a priceless gem, she held the knowledge at arm's length and examined it against the light, marveling at its sparkling facets. It was too brilliant. Her eyes couldn't stand the brightness. She pushed the thought aside. Her future was too uncertain.

"I shouldn't have told you about the marriage," she said in a moment.

"You didn't tell me, remember? I already knew." The wagon paused on the edge of the stream. He clucked to the horses, and the buckboard rattled down the bank. "There's a verse in Proverbs says, 'Trust in the Lord with all thine heart; and lean not unto thine own understanding. In all thy ways acknowledge him, and he shall direct thy paths.' You've been trying to carry the load your ownself, Miss Megan. Give the problem to Jesus. The Lord will take care of the future."

❧

Letting the Lord take care of the future wasn't always easy as windy and cold October became icy November. True, Jeremy was better. With the help of a kind nurse, Em sent glowing letters that thrilled Megan. Jeremy was able to sit in chair for an hour at a time now. He gained strength by the day.

In spite of the good news, the feeling of emptiness lingered. Since her talk with Banjo, Megan was intensely aware of Steve. It was exhilarating torture. Secretly she scrutinized his every word, every expression hoping vainly for a sign that he cared for her. He was polite, even deferential, but no more.

When the feeble light of a frigid November morning crept into the kitchen, she parted the curtain to see snow silently sifting down from a steel sky. The roof of the stable was covered in downy white, and little mounds were forming on top of each aspen post of the corral. Excited, she dropped the curtain and ran to the front windows to look at the meadow, fast disappearing under a fluffy, cold blanket.

"It's snowing!" she called to Steve when she heard the scuffling of his boots overhead. "It's snowing!" Happy as a child on Christmas morning she skipped about the kitchen, popping a pan of biscuits into the oven, stirring the oatmeal with flourish.

The snow fell for three days, filling the meadow until not one nubby corn stalk could be seen and forming white winter blossoms on the trees. The house was tolerably warm as long as the fireplace blazed and the kitchen stove glowed. Megan despaired of ever being able to keep the kitchen linoleum clean with the constant tracking in of snow-laden boots from the stack of wood behind the house.

Because of the bitter cold Lobo stayed in the stable with the horses and Banjo's potbelly stove, but every day Megan disappeared under wool wraps, scarves, and mittens to walk with him in the yard. She scattered crumbs for the ravenous birds and then knelt down to study their star-shaped tracks in the snow, wishing there was some way to preserve such a pristine art. She and Lobo played and ran until numb feet and chattering teeth forced her back to the throbbing, aching warmth of the roaring fireplace.

On the morning of the second day Megan was surprised when Steve came into the kitchen while she was washing the breakfast dishes.

"I want to make a built-in sideboard in the dining room. I was wondering where you thought would be the best place to put it."

She stood on the edge of the room taking stock of the oak table and the two windows.

"Why don't you put it in the corner? The depth of the corner would make extra storage space without taking so much space from the room."

"Good idea." He walked to the corner and spread his hands. "From here to here?" He nodded, considering. "And a small cabinet overhead with glassed-in doors for pretty dishes would be nice, too, wouldn't it?"

"That would be nice."

"I've been saving some wood for the project. It's in the stable. We may as well use up all this empty time doing something useful." Shrugging into their heavy coats, he and Banjo went out the back door and came back carrying some wide pine boards. They moved the table into the living room and soon the air was filled with the rasping noise of sawing interrupted by loud pounding.

"Never use nails on furniture," Banjo said philosophically as he whittled a peg. "Like the Good Book advises, you don't put new wine in old bottles. Well, you don't put iron nails in good furniture."

"That your interpretation?" Steve asked, smiling.

"Sure, from the book of Banjo Calahan." Banjo chuckled. "You know, Chamberlin, the Good Book does have plenty to say about life that's for our good. It's not just for women and old folks. Like in Isaiah, 'Though your sins be as scarlet, they shall be as white as snow,' or in Matthew 'I am not come to call the righteous, but sinners to repentance.' "

Steve picked up the saw and drew it loudly across a board. Smiling to himself, Banjo picked up another scrap of wood to whittle.

"Haven't you ever thought about your soul?" Banjo continued when Steve lay down the saw.

"Not much." Steve gave Banjo a calculating look.

"You ought to. Young fellow like you has a long future ahead of him. Jesus can make all the difference as to how things come out."

"That your sermon for today?" Steve asked, mildly, picking up the hand drill.

Megan heard their conversation from the kitchen. "Please, God," she prayed, "convince him that he needs You."

If only Steve were a Christian. Maybe then things would be different.

The men were still working on the cabinet when she sat down to write a letter to Jeremy. She wanted to tell him about the snow. If he were able to be here he'd be rolling in the cold whiteness with Lobo, his cheeks ruddy with good health and a happy, secure life.

What would happen to them when she went back to Baltimore? Another squalid tenement house? She shuddered. How could she go back to the city now? "Oh God," she prayed, "help me to trust and leave the rest to You."

❧

The weather warmed up a little after two weeks of near-zero temperatures. The snow melted, leaving the ground soggy. Great puddle lakes lay across the meadow. Cold, damp, and miserable, Steve and Banjo slogged back to the house after the evening choring.

"I believe I like the snow better than the slush," Steve remarked, warming his hands before the fireplace. "This dampness goes plumb through a body."

"Soup's ready," Megan called from the kitchen. Hot food warmed their insides and cheered the men considerably. They were lingering over steaming cups of black coffee, enjoying the peacefulness of the evening when a commotion in the stable broke off the conversation. Lobo was barking frantically, loud, angry barks with no letup. A horse gave a piercing whinny and there was the scuffling noise of pawing hoofs.

"Smoke!" An acrid smell and the scream of a horse reached Megan the same time as Banjo's cry.

"The stable! The stable's on fire!" Banjo overturned his chair in his hurry to reach the back door.

On the run, Steve grabbed his gunbelt from its peg and followed him.

"Get the stock behind the house," Steve called as they banged out the back door. "And if Harrington's men are out there, heaven help 'em if I get my sights on one of 'em." The back door crashed closed, and they were gone.

From the kitchen window Megan could see smoke billowing from the far side of the stable. She grabbed the water bucket from the counter and ran to the back door in time to see Steve struggling to get panic-stricken Candy out of the stable.

"Steady, girl," Megan called, soothingly. "Steady, girl." She set down the bucket and walked slowly toward the horse.

Candy turned her head in Megan's direction and nickered. Holding her hand out, Megan walked on until she held the horse's bridle.

"Tie her to the side of the spring house," Steve called and ran back inside the stable. Banjo led Kelsey and Bess out as Megan drew Candy along. The presence of the other stock calmed the mare, and Megan was able to tie her without any difficulty.

Billy and Star bounded from the smoke-filled stable, their eyes rolling in terror, making it hard for Steve to keep them from rearing up. Tying them with hasty fingers, Steve raced back to the stable as Caesar's screams rose to a crescendo. Banjo held the horse's halter. He had to step nimbly to avoid the gelding's flying hooves.

"Megan, get in the house!" Steve yelled. He grabbed the halter on the other side so he and Banjo could force the horse into the fenced-in corridor. Thrashing and heaving, Caesar fought them. His front hoof caught Banjo on the leg, throwing him to the ground. Steve held on with both hands, talking, pleading with the horse. The fire roared higher behind them. Rearing high, Caesar raised Steve off the ground then bolted, dragging Steve along.

"Let him go!" Banjo shouted. "He'll kill you!"

Throwing himself clear, Steve fell into the freezing water of the stone basin. Caesar bounded forward toward the only opening he could see, and he galloped headlong over the cliff. His terrified scream turned Megan's blood to ice.

Teeth chattering, limbs shaking, Steve walked to the edge of the house and looked down. He stayed there only an instant.

"It's-s as black as pitch-ch down there," he stuttered, coming back. "I c-can't see a thing." He walked past Megan to where Banjo lay. The air was thick with heavy smoke and the hissing and popping of burning wood. Inside the stable a heavy timber crashed to the ground.

"You've got to get into some dry clothes or you'll freeze," Megan cried after him. She raised an arm to shield her eyes from the smoke, blinking as she peered after Steve.

"The f-fire will keep me from freezing. We've got to s-stop the flames from reaching the house."

"I'll help you tear down the fence." Banjo struggled to his feet.

"Chamberlin!" Beau Harrington's adolescent voice called from the darkness. "This is just the beginning, Chamberlin. Next it'll be the house. Or better yet, we'll string you up to the highest cottonwood around. Won't we, Turner?"

"Turner!" Steve's voice bellowed above the roar of the inferno. "I know you, Turner. Come out in the open, you yellow dog, and fight like a man!"

"It would be your funeral, Chamberlin." A second voice called back. "No two-bit riverboat gambler could hold a candle to me!"

"Keep talking, Turner. I've almost got it."

"Got what?" The voice was edgy.

"Your real name. It'll come to me sooner or later."

The only answer he received was the volley of pounding hoofbeats retreating across the meadow.

eighteen

With strength that came from desperation, they tugged and tore at the smoldering wooden fence until there was a sizable gap between the house and the stable. Without a thought for her bruised, scraped hands, Megan worked on. Hauling bucket after bucket of water, they drenched the fence and the side of the house, praying all the while the wind would not blow in their direction.

"The chickens!" Megan cried. "What about the chickens?"

"I think the coop is far enough from the stable to be out of danger," Steve said, wiping his smoke-bleary eyes with his sleeve, "but I'll go open the door so they can get out just in case."

The roof of the stable collapsed with a jarring, scraping crash, sending a shower of sparks into the black sky. It startled Megan and broke the last thread of her endurance. She walked over to Candy and leaned forward, resting her head on the mare's neck. She didn't want Steve to see her, but she couldn't hold in tears any longer.

"Come." Steve's hand was on her arm. "Let's go inside. You're all in."

Megan washed the smeary soot from her face and set on the coffeepot. Steve climbed to the loft in search of dry clothes while Banjo hobbled in, painfully favoring his right leg, and sat down at the table.

"Is your leg, okay?" Megan asked, worried.

"It will be in a day or two. It's just bruised. We can thank the good Lord no one was hurt any worse tonight. Trying to get a spooked horse out of a burning building is dangerous work. Your husband is a brave man."

Megan felt tears welling up again, hot, furious, revengeful tears. The hay and fodder they had carefully stored were gone as well as the buckboard and saddles. With six animals to feed through the winter the loss was devastating.

"I could find it in myself to hate Beau Harrington," she said as she brought the coffeepot and three cups to the table. She sank into a chair and put her hands over her face.

"I know how you feel, Miss Megan," Banjo replied. "Just you remember, the Lord doesn't play any favorites when it comes to sin. Our sin is just as wicked in His sight as Beau's."

"I can't understand how anyone could be so vicious. We have a deed to this property. We've never done anything to hurt the Harringtons. We're right and they're wrong. So why are we the ones suffering?"

"I don't claim to understand it myself. All I know is that boy needs the Lord. Just the same as you and me."

"I guess you'll have to take the loft, Banjo," Steve said, later. "No doubt it'll be more comfortable than the stable was."

"I'm much obliged." Banjo said slowly. He bent over to rub a spot below the knee. "But I don't know if I can climb the ladder." He took two steps, testing his leg. "I'd best bed down in front of the fireplace tonight." He looked at Megan. "That is if you have an extra blanket."

"Oh, Banjo," Megan cried, "all your things were in the stable. You didn't even mention it. Of course I have a blanket. And anything else you need."

"Beggin' your pardon, ma'am, my Sharps was in the house, and Kelsey's safe out back. Long as I've got them and the Lord that's all I need. The only thing I regret is my Bible. It's been with me since I got out of the army. I rode nigh two hundred miles to get it. But I'll get another'n one day." He sank to a chair, his face tense as he eased his leg.

"I'll get the blanket right away." Megan hurried to her room for the blanket, wondering at Banjo's matter-of-fact attitude through this entire ordeal.

"Why don't you let me have a look at the leg?" she asked as she arranged the blanket on the couch. "I may be able to do something for it, you know."

"Just let it rest tonight, Miss Megan."

"Megan's a hand when it comes to doctorin'," Steve said, coming to stand near her, close enough for his arm to brush hers.

"Tomorrow," Banjo insisted. "All I want now is a little rest." He lay down, rolled up in the blanket, and was still.

Megan rinsed out the coffee cups. Her mind was fuzzy with fatigue, her body weary beyond the point of exhaustion. She traced her way to her room hardly aware of her surroundings, but she turned around, startled, when she heard Steve follow her inside.

"How are we going to handle having Banjo in here?" he whispered after firmly shutting the door. He glanced at the floor. "I don't relish the thought of sleeping on the floor for the duration of the winter."

"I'm afraid I have something to confess." Megan avoided his gaze. She was afraid what she had to tell him would make him angry. "Banjo knows. About us, I mean."

"What?" His brows drew together.

"He's all right. He won't tell anyone. I was upset one day and he asked me about it. I guess I just blurted it all out." She turned away from his frown. "I know I shouldn't have. If it was anyone else, even Susan, I wouldn't have told. But Banjo's different."

Steve studied her a moment before his expression relaxed.

"I guess it's just as well under the circumstances. You're right on two counts. You shouldn't have told. And Banjo is different. I've never met anyone like him." He pulled his gun from its holster and checked the load. "I've got to see about Caesar. I can't let him lie down there with a broken leg or worse to suffer through the night." He put his hand on the door latch. "I couldn't rest if I did."

Megan crawled between the stiff, cold sheets and lay back with a deep sigh. Her eyes were so heavy she expected to drop off to sleep right away. Her eyes stayed closed but sleep didn't come, for her ears were straining, her mind wondering what Steve would find at the bottom of the cliff.

She must have dozed, because the sound of a single shot jerked her awake, and made her heart race. When the awful reality came to her, she turned her face into her pillow and wept.

෬

Shivering with cold, Megan hurried into her clothes before dawn the next morning. With shaking hands she added small logs to the glowing orange coals in the kitchen stove and put on the coffeepot. Banjo hadn't moved when she tiptoed past, so she worked quietly, trying not to waken him.

She mixed the pancake batter, set it aside for frying when the men were ready, and sliced bacon into a pan. A quick glance out the kitchen window stopped her in midmotion and made her go back for a longer look. Before her lay the blackened, still-smoldering remains of the stable. It was nothing more than a flattened heap of rubble with the old potbelly stove standing toward the back. Across the yard the chickens hopped in and out of the open door of the henhouse scratching and pecking about.

Megan tore herself away from the window when she heard Steve's tread on the loft ladder. She added coffee grounds to the boiling pot and set the cast-iron skillet on the stove.

"Sleep okay?" Steve pulled a chair from the table and sat down. Dark circles rimmed his bloodshot eyes.

"Well enough." She greased the skillet with a piece of bacon and poured on some pancake batter.

"I had to put Caesar away." He ran his hand through his hair. "Both front legs were broken."

"I heard." When the first pancake was done she added a little cold water to the brewing coffee. Filling a thick, white mug to the brim, she set it on the table in front of Steve.

"I've got to ride over to Hohner's spread to see it he'll loan me a wagon and if he can sell me some hay for the stock. Buying feed is going to take most of our profit from the corn crop," he added, bitterly.

"What about making a profit to meet the terms of the will?"

"We still have the cattle. If I have to I'll sell them all in the spring. We'll still get by." He hit a hard fist on the table top. "If I had that Beau Harrington where I could get at him. . . ." His eyes narrowed. "Not only him. That Turner fellow. I was awake most of the night trying to remember how I know him. I finally figured it out.

"He was in the Confederate army. But his name wasn't Turner, it was Taylor. Charlie Taylor.

"He joined our outfit outside of Chattanooga. We used to pass the time playing poker for pennies when we had them, or else we used match sticks. Anyway, we were having a friendly game and my friend, Ted Miller, was winning. The boys used to kid me about being a riverboat gambler and losing to Ted, who was a farm boy." He stared into space, absently running his forefinger along the rim of his coffee cup.

"Ted and Charlie were the only two left in the game when Ted showed three aces. Charlie was mad as hops. Stood up and called Ted a cheat. Well, Ted pulled a knife and they set to. Like magic, Charlie had a knife in his hand, too. I never did figure out where he got it from.

"They came at each other and Ted cut Charlie a bad one on his cheek. Ted stepped back and about that time Charlie flipped that shiv to where he held it by the tip and threw it right into Ted's heart. Ted dropped like a stone. I don't think he even knew what hit him."

"What happened to Charlie?"

"They took him to the hospital. We pulled out shortly after that, and I never saw him again."

"Did he know you could use a knife?" She piled three pancakes on a plate and brought them to the table with a jar of sorghum.

"Come to think of it, he probably did. We used to practice pitching sometimes. He could have seen me. Offhand I can't remember ever holding a conversation with the man. That's why it took me so long to place him." He poured a generous amount of sorghum on the pancakes and ate like a man with an appetite.

"I'll ride Billy bareback to Hohner's," Steve said later as he set a pail of Bess's milk on the counter. "Should be back well before noon."

"Please be careful," Megan pleaded. "They'd have no scruples about ambushing you if they could."

"You watch yourself," Banjo called from the table where he

was finishing a piece of bacon.

Later, Megan was wrapping Banjo's bruised shin in brown paper and vinegar when the drumming of a running horse drew her to the front window. Riding a horse Megan had never seen before, Susan raced into the dooryard. She wore a brown coat and her Sunday bonnet.

Megan threw open the door to catch the panting young woman by the arm and draw her inside.

"What's happened?" Megan demanded, fear overtaking her.

"It's Beau," Susan gasped. "He's getting the men in town stirred up about Pa's murder. They're organizing a lynching party to come after Steve."

"Sit down, child," Banjo commanded. "Get hold of yourself, so you can tell us the rest."

Susan pulled at the buttons on her coat until she managed to get it off and hand it to Megan. Her hands trembled as she struggled to untie the strings on her bonnet. She sat in a chair near the blazing fireplace. Her breathing was more regular, but panic lingered beneath the surface.

"Beau took some of the hands into town this morning. They kept laughing and saying they were going to celebrate. I couldn't understand it all." She clenched her white hands in her lap.

"I went along to see Mrs. Mullins, who has a new baby. I think the men had already been drinking a little from the way they were acting." She shuddered. "When I came out of the Mullins's house I saw a commotion in front of the Gold Mine Saloon. Beau was standing on a barrel in front of the crowd. I walked close enough to hear him call out that Steve Chamberlin had killed Pa. Clyde Turner got a rope off his saddle horn and held it up." She squeezed her eyes shut. "It was awful. When I saw what they were up to I ran to the telegraph office and asked Tom to wire Denver for the marshal, then I ran back to Mrs. Mullins and borrowed a horse. I had come in with Beau in the buckboard."

"What are we going to do?" Megan asked Banjo.

"Sit tight until Steve gets back. He'll be here directly." He pulled the paper off his leg. "In the meantime, bring me my

Sharps." He pulled down his pants leg and stood holding the back of the chair. "I'll set by the window and keep an eye on things."

"Mrs. Mullins loaned me a Winchester," Susan said.

"You wouldn't fight against your own brother!" Megan was horrified.

"Don't count on it." Susan's mouth was set in a hard line. "After all I've been through with him in the past few months, I'd be likely to do just about anything."

Megan dug every bit of ammunition from the kitchen cabinet and set the boxes on the sideboard. She took the Henry from the wall and lay it beside the bullets.

"May as well put on some more coffee and fix some vittles," Banjo said. "It's hard tellin' how long it'll take them to get here." Holding the rifle across his lap he stared out the window. "They'll probably stop at the saloon and drink to their plan before headin' out. Bunch of coyotes."

"Here comes Steve in a buckboard full of hay," he announced an hour later. "Looks like he did right well for hisself. Hohner let him have another horse to help pull it."

Steve pulled the buckboard behind the standing length of fence. He climbed into the back of the wagon to throw hay to the stock before coming in the back door.

"Beau Harrington is stirring up a lynch mob in Juniper to come after you. Susan rode out to warn us," Megan blurted out from the back door.

"How many?" Steve asked, stepping past her into the house. He walked to the sideboard and looked at the weaponry spread there.

"Twenty-five or thirty if they all come," Susan said, quietly.

"She wired for the marshal," Banjo said, "but it'll take him a day to get here."

"We'll have to stand them off." He loaded the empty chamber in his six-shooter, snapped the magazine shut, and replaced it in his holster. Striding to the ladder, he brought his other pistol down and loaded it. A strained, suspenseful silence saturated the room. Megan, preparing lunch, wondered how long she could stand the tension. Had the fire been only yesterday?

nineteen

"Here they come!" Banjo's words late that afternoon brought everyone to his feet. Clutching her rifle, Megan took up her post by the living room window, heart racing, mouth dry. She looked past the edge of the window to see a small group of riders enter the clearing. They rode close together. Beau's pinto was in the lead.

"When they get in range, dust them," Steve ordered calmly.

Raising the window a small crack, Megan knelt and rested her rifle on the sill. To her, the men outside were no longer fellow human beings; they had become the enemy who wanted to destroy what she loved. Swallowing hard, she took up the slack under the trigger and waited. She heard Lobo's excited bark near the front of the house.

"Now!" A volley of shots rang out at Steve's command.

As one man the group wheeled and ran for the shelter of the trees. There were a few answering shots then all was still.

"Don't let them fool you; they're still there." Banjo eased his leg as he leaned forward. "I wonder how cold they'll have to get before they give up."

But they didn't give up. After an hour of waiting, a thin plume of gray smoke rose above the trees.

"They've built themselves a fire," Steve commented. "Looks like they'll be staying a while."

"Long's we've got food and ammunition, we'll be all right. The law will be here directly," Banjo said, dryly.

"What if the marshal won't listen to us?" Megan spoke for the first time.

"He'll listen," Steve answered. "That Walker's a square dealer. He doesn't want to hang the wrong man."

"I hope you are right," Megan answered doubtfully.

"Let's take turns watching, Banjo," Steve said, stretching. "No need for all of us to watch all night. I don't think they'll be doing anything drastic right away."

Shortly after dark, Lobo's barking intensified. He was behind the house now.

"Call off the dog!" A young man's voice called from the stable ruins. "I'm coming to join you."

"It's Wyatt!" Susan cried, running for the back door. Megan was closer. She unbolted the door and called, "Down, Lobo!" Lobo growled softly, the fur on his back standing up. "It's okay. Wyatt's a friend." The canine trotted to Megan and put his wet nose under her hand.

Susan slipped past Megan and raced to Wyatt. She threw herself at him with such force he stepped back, off balance.

"Now that's what I call a welcome!" He put his arm around Susan's shoulder. "And what, may I ask, are you doing here?" He guided her inside the house.

"I came to warn them this morning when I saw what Beau was up to."

"So that's where you went off to." He squeezed her gently. "I was powerful worried about you when you disappeared.

"Chamberlin," he turned to Steve, "I ride for the brand, but there comes a time when a man has to stand for what's right. What Harrington's doing is right lowdown, and I can't abide it any longer." He looked down at Susan. "Are you with me?"

"I've always been with you." She smiled tremulously up at him.

"What are they planning to do?" Steve asked.

"The gang? They don't really have no plan. Just starve you out as far as I know. Beau and some of the hands were pretty bad off for liquor when I left. And the rest were getting tired. They'll probably sleep it off until early morning unless someone gets a bright idea before then.

"This place is a fortress. It's almost impossible to get within shooting range without getting shot first. I slid in on my belly right next to the rock face, but I doubt any of them are that determined. Might ought to keep a watch thataway, though."

"Lobo will keep watch," Steve replied.

Wyatt and Susan settled on the sofa in the flickering glow of the fireplace, the only light in the room. Steve relieved Banjo at the window, and Megan tried to keep from nodding as the heat from the fire relaxed her weary muscles. Hands clasped under his head, Banjo stretched out on his back before the hearth.

"This is cozy as a goose in a corncrib," Banjo drawled. "It'll be good havin' another man to spell us with the watching." He looked over at Wyatt. "Feel up to takin' the next round?" Suddenly, his expression changed. He stared at Wyatt's feet stretched out, ankles crossed, before him.

"Sure. I can take it." Wyatt noticed Banjo's wrinkled brow. "What's the matter?"

"Where'd you get those boots?"

"Bought them in Cheyenne this spring. There's an old timer up there who makes them." He looked down at the feathery pattern stamped on the light brown leather. "Why?"

"Were you wearin' 'em the night Harrington was killed?"

"I reckon." He sat up straighter. "I've worn 'em to all the occasions since I got them." He stopped. "Wait a minute. Wait. . . a. . .minute." He stared overhead. "I didn't wear them that night. I hadn't intended on going because I was sick all day. Clyde Turner broke the heel off his good boots. We're about the same size, so I told him to go ahead and wear mine. Then I got to feeling better. I hated to disappoint Susan so I shined up my old black boots and went anyway. I let Clyde have my new ones. I didn't want to take them back after I told him he could have them."

"I found those boot prints at the edge of the clearing where Harrington was killed," Banjo explained. "More than likely the man who wore them killed Harrington. The murderer stood there a while, dropped a green juniper twig he'd been chewing, and stepped out like you do if you're throwing a knife."

"You mean Clyde Turner was wearing those boots that night?" Steve spoke from the window.

"Does he chew green juniper twigs?" Megan asked, now wide awake.

"He chews some kind of wood. I don't rightly know if it's juniper or not. I never looked close." Wyatt looked around. "You think Clyde did it? Why would he do a fool thing like that?"

"We haven't put it all together yet," Steve said, "but I think we're finally barking up the right tree."

"Well, I'll be." Wyatt propped his right ankle on his left knee. "You may have a loop on the right steer at that. He sure has been coming off all high and mighty since Harrington died. Especially with the hands."

"He makes me feel creepy inside." Susan moved even closer to Wyatt.

ᕯ

Before daylight the next morning Megan broke the thin layer of ice on her wash basin and bathed her face to drive sleep from her eyes. She had left Susan sleeping in the bedroom to stir up the fire in the kitchen stove, add a few small logs, and set on the coffeepot.

"Been a long night," Steve commented from his post. His face was grizzled, his hair tousled. Only his keen eyes seemed the same as they had been last night when she had finally gone to bed. Wyatt stretched out on the floor, and Banjo snored softly on the sofa.

"Coffee'll be ready soon." She pulled the flour bin from under the counter. "If that'll help." She smiled in his direction.

"Having someone to talk to helps." He leaned back, resting an elbow on the back of his chair. "I took over for Banjo about two hours ago. Nothing's moving out there as far as I can tell."

"I hope we don't have to pass another night like last night." She scooped some flour into a large bowl. "What are we going to do?"

"I'm not planning on being the main attraction at any neck stretching party. I can tell you that." He rotated his shoulders, working out the kinks. "If we have to fight, we'll fight. If the marshal comes, and we can convince him I'm innocent, we'll do that."

It was a haggard crew that gathered at the breakfast table at dawn. Susan's face was strained, her eyes seemed too large for her thin face. She hovered near Wyatt, speaking little and glancing often toward the front windows. Megan bustled about setting on the oatmeal, biscuits, and bacon more from the need to stay busy than from any need to hurry.

"With your permission, Chamberlin," Banjo said as they sat to the table, "I feel the need to ask the good Lord's help during this day. Would you mind if I said a short prayer before we ate?"

"Help yourself, Banjo. We can use all the help we can get."

Megan watched Steve closely to see if he was making light of Banjo's request, but his face was expressionless, his eyes serious. He bowed his head, studying the edge of the table while Banjo prayed.

"Dear Lord, we know You have a reason for everythin' that comes into our lives. I pray that You would watch over us today. Protect us from harm and teach us all to trust in You. Amen."

A dreadful lethargy caused by weariness and anxiety hovered over the stone house that morning. Conversation lagged. Everyone was too consumed with his own thoughts and fears for small talk. The sun was high above the horizon before the long-awaited something happened.

"Chamberlin! Come on out. I want to talk to you. It's Ben Walker, the marshal."

"It may be a trick." Megan took a step in Steve's direction.

"That's Walker's voice all right." Steve peered out the window, keeping his body behind the stone wall. "I can see him. He's astride his horse to the north of the meadow. The gang is behind him."

"Yes, sir, Mr. Walker," Steve called back. "But I'm keeping my guns."

"Keep them. I only want to talk to you."

Megan could scarcely breathe as she watched Steve check his guns, slide them loosely in their holsters, and walk to the door. Putting on his hat and buffalo coat, he went out. Swiftly putting on her wrap and picking up her Henry, she shoved a handful of shells into her pocket and followed him. Banjo had already stepped through the door ahead of her, buffalo gun in hand.

Banjo stopped five yards behind and to the right of Steve at the edge of the dooryard. Megan stood a few feet from Banjo. She could feel her pulse pounding in her neck. Her eyes were riveted to the men in front of them.

Megan sensed someone walking up behind her. She turned to see Wyatt pass by her and stand a few feet to her left, his shooting iron ready. Susan stood on the edge of the porch huddled in her coat, looking small and helpless. But the rifle she held was neither small nor helpless.

twenty

"There he is, Marshal! Take him!" His breath billowing out in white clouds as he spoke, Beau stepped his horse ahead of the ten to fifteen men behind the lawman. Their number had diminished considerably during the freezing night.

"That's high-handed talk comin' from a fellow whose sister stands with the other side," Banjo remarked, dryly. His voice, though not loud, carried far in the icy air.

"The rest of you brave hombres are hangin' far back for men acting in the cause of justice," Banjo continued. His voice was thick with sarcasm. "You, Harper." The storekeeper jerked his head around at the sound of his name. "Are you here because you think Chamberlin's guilty, or because it's Harrington money that keeps you in business?

"And Jim Sanders. If Chamberlin were hung for the murder of Harrington it would take suspicion off you, wouldn't it?" Sanders studied the ground. "Everyone remembers the old score you had with Harrington." Banjo's eyes shifted to the two hulking figures in the rear.

"I can't say I'm surprised to see you, Henry. Al. You know where your bread's buttered, don't you?" As each man heard his name, there was a marked change of attitude. The thought uppermost in each man's mind was how to bow out without losing face.

"Marshal, I'd like to swear out a warrant," Steve said.

"You'd like to swear out a warrant?" Beau's look was lethal enough to kill a rabbit at twenty yards.

"Quiet, Harrington," Walker ordered. "Let him have his say."

"I'd like to swear out a warrant on Clyde Turner, otherwise known as Charlie Taylor, on suspicion of the murder of Victor Harrington."

Turner stiffened. He slowly took from his mouth the twig he was chewing.

"He's talking through his hat, Marshal," Turner said easily, back on balance again.

"Check that twig he has in his hand," Steve countered. "How many men do you know that chews juniper?" He reminded Walker of the twig found at the Running M after the murder and told him of the matching twig found at the campsite near the Hohner range.

In a furtive movement, Turner flicked the twig he held away from him.

Sanders saw what Turner was up to and slid from the saddle to pick up the twig. He handed it to Walker.

"You've got to be crazy," Turner said, angrily. "Why would I want to kill my own boss?"

"Maybe because he was getting too close to catching you rustling his cattle," Steve said. "Right, Henry?" Henry Hohner's jaw dropped open, his buckteeth sticking out. Seeing his reaction, Steve plowed on. "We found that pretty little box canyon on the Hohner range. The perfect place to hide stolen cattle until time to take them to the railroad. You boys had a real nice setup, didn't you?"

"It wasn't us!" Panic-stricken, Al spoke up. His eyes turned toward Turner. "All we did was pick up a few cows and keep them hid away. He did all the rest," he babbled, jerking his horse's head back as he sawed the reins.

"You idiot!" Furious, Turner railed at Al, the scar twitching as he spoke. "Don't you know what he's doing? He's trying to trap you into admitting something."

"Turner's knife slick, Walker," Steve continued. "I knew him in the war. His real name's Charlie Taylor. I saw him throw a knife and kill a man. It took me a while to place him because of that scar. But I know him all right. If you look a little deeper I believe you'll find he's been prodding young Harrington and fomenting the trouble we've had between us."

"He's right, Marshal." It was Curly, the bald, Rocking H hand that spoke up this time. "I've heard Turner making hints and pushing young Harrington. Us boys have had about all we kin take. I say he's your man." He walked his horse across the field to Steve and turned around, watching Clyde Turner carefully.

Slowly, thoughtfully, Slim and two others joined him.

"I don't know about the rest of you folks," Sanders said, turning his horse, "but I'm heading home. I can smell a polecat when I get next to one."

Turner cast an ugly glance in his direction.

Pointedly ignoring him, Sanders prodded his horse to a trot. The rest of the townsfolk followed, leaving Beau and Turner alone with Marshal Walker in the meadow.

"Stay where you are, Turner." The lawman's revolver was in his hand. "You're riding back with me. I'll get your accomplices, by and by. Right now I want you." He took Turner's guns, pulled two pigging strings from his saddle, and tied Turner's hands to the pommel.

"I should have killed you, Chamberlin!" Stark hatred glared from Turner's weasel face. "I should have killed you when I first recognized you. You are the only one who knew who I was. I tried on the trail, but I missed. All I did was burn your horse and see if he'd do the job. If I had made that shot I could have had it all. The Rocking H and everything that goes with it."

"Your days are over, Turner." Steve spoke without rancor. "There's no place here for your kind."

Beau had not uttered a sound throughout the unfolding of the facts about his father's death. He watched the marshal take Turner away as though he couldn't quite understand what was happening.

"Kill him, Beau!" Clyde Turner yelled in a desperate try for revenge. "Kill Chamberlin! He's the cause of all your trouble! Kill him!"

Marshal Walker silenced Turner with a lash of his quirt. He grabbed the reins of Turner's horse, and they trotted into the trees.

Absently looking at the spot where they disappeared, Beau was as still as though carved in marble. The four Rocking H hands slowly followed the marshal. Wyatt returned to Susan on the steps. Their footsteps and the creak of the door told Megan they had gone inside. Banjo relaxed, resting his rifle in the crook of his arm, barrel down. He stepped forward to meet Steve as they broke ranks. Megan, too, stepped forward. But a movement caught her eye. Looking back she stopped dead in her tracks, horror gripping her.

It happened in an instant, a split second. There was no time to cry out, no time to warn Steve. There was only time for action. Totally by reflex, Megan raised her rifle to her shoulder as Beau Harrington sighted his Winchester at Steve. Their shots, only a fraction of a second apart, sounded as one.

But Megan was too late.

Beau dropped his rifle and grabbed his right biceps, but Megan had already forgotten him. She had eyes only for Steve sprawled on the snowy ground before her, a thick red stain spreading from a point just above the knee of his left leg. Banjo already kneeled beside him.

"Get a cloth to tie around his leg to stop the bleeding!" he ordered.

Megan pulled her handkerchief from her sleeve. Quickly Banjo tore the thin white cloth in half, tied the ends together, and wrapped it tightly around Steve's thigh. He and Wyatt carried him, half-conscious, to Megan's room where they put him on the bed.

Steve's eyelids fluttered. He opened them wide and tried to sit up.

He fell back with a groan. "What happened?"

"That fool boy Harrington shot you in the leg," Banjo said between tense lips. He stepped aside so Megan could cut away Steve's trouser leg with a small pair of scissors. "Wyatt's going for Doc Leatherwood." He laid his hand gently on Megan's arm. "You know what to do. I'd best go have a look at the boy out yonder."

Megan didn't answer. She was only conscious that the bleeding must be stopped. She was terrified that the bone might be broken. She raced for a bowl full of flour from the bin. Taking a handful of flour, she packed the wounds, front and back, and wrapped the leg tightly with a wide strip hurriedly cut from a sheet. Susan's sobs reached her from the living room, but she paid no mind. There would be time for Susan later.

Rushing to the closet, she found the paper of powder given

her by the doctor for the pain in her shoulder. She poured a generous portion into a glass, mixed it with a little water, and held it to Steve's lips.

"What's that?" he grimaced, then shivered.

"For the pain." She smoothed his hair back from his pain-creased brow.

There's so little I can do, she agonized. *If something happens to him, how can I go on without him?*

She remembered the sound of his anxious voice calling her name when she was lying on the ground beside the overturned buckboard. She thought about his strong arm around her, supporting her on that torturous journey home. His insistence on getting Jeremy better care. Their quiet walks and talks beside the lake. He was security, comfort, and happiness to her as she had never known before.

With unspeakable dread she watched the crimson stain spreading over the bandage.

"Please, God," she begged with all her being, "stop the bleeding and let him get well. I know it may be selfish, but I can't face life without him."

Yet, even as she prayed she knew she would face life without him next spring.

She walked into the living room when she heard the front door close.

It was Banjo. "How is he?"

"Dozing off and on. I gave him some of the pain powder I had left." She wrung her hands. "How long until the doctor can get here?"

"It could be another two hours, it could be tonight. There's no way of tellin'." He pulled off his coat and hung it on a peg. "Your brother's not hurt bad, Miss Susan." On the sofa, leaning against the back, Susan lifted a red, puffy face from her arm. Her breath came in ragged sobs. "He only got a flesh wound in his upper arm," Banjo told her.

"I didn't intend on killing him," Megan said, reasonably. "I figured if I shot his gun arm it would stop him."

Eyebrows raised, Banjo stared.

"You intended on shootin' his arm?"

"Yes. Why?"

"Well, I'll be a jack rabbit's hind leg. It must have been a hundred yards."

"Where is he?" Susan stood and leaned to look out the window.

"He was on the ground trying to get a grip on his Winchester when I went out. He was whining like a baby. Somehow he'd managed to get his bandanna tied around the wound. I tried to help him, but he swore at me and knocked my hand away. Didn't say where he was headed, but he was in a big hurry to get there."

"I'm sorry, Susan." Megan put her hand on her friend's shoulder.

"I'm not upset about that. Beau got what he's been asking for. It's hearing about Pa's murder that's got me upset. To think that Clyde Turner was the one. Just remembering all the times I was near him makes my insides turn over."

The doctor arrived shortly after noon. With haunted eyes Megan watched him unwrap the wounded leg.

"How bad is it, Doc?" Steve asked through thin, white lips.

"I've seen worse." After cleansing the wounds, Dr. Leatherwood made a close inspection. "I doubt that the bone is broken, but you'll have to take it real easy on the leg for a month or so." He smiled at Megan. "It's a good thing your wife knew how to stop the bleeding so soon. If she follows my instructions as well as that you should be up and around before long." He rebandaged the leg, gave Steve another dose of powder, and stepped outside for a word with Megan.

"You did fine." He nodded appreciatively to Megan as Banjo looked on. "I'm glad the bullet passed clean through. The wound will drain better, and we won't have to go through the ordeal of digging out a bullet. Change the bandage and put on antiseptic twice a day to try to ward off any infection. That's the biggest danger. Infection. Here's some more of that powder. Don't give it to him unless he needs it, but he'll be needing it for the next two or three days." He put on his hat. "I'll be back around to see him day after tomorrow."

The doctor's words eased Megan's fears a little, but the

possibility of infection was an ugly specter hovering over the sick man's bed. Megan had to force herself to leave him long enough to do a minimum of cooking and washing. She wanted to be with him every second.

~

"I've been a fool," Steve said tersely through the pain the next day.

Concerned, Megan felt his forehead before answering.

"No, I'm not delirious," he said, ruefully. "I'm thinking more clearly than I have for years." Beads of sweat stood out on his forehead. Megan wiped them away with a cool cloth. "A few inches higher and I'd have been a goner, Megan. It's put me to thinking about what my life means. If it's really important." He took a sip from the glass she offered him.

"You're tiring yourself by talking so much," she cautioned.

"I've got to tell you this," he insisted with an impatient wave of his hand, "so don't stop me." He paused while she pulled a chair close to his bed. "I guess I've been turning it over in my mind for a long time, but it never struck me as so important until now. I'm talking about my standing with God. Like you and Banjo have been trying to tell me. I want to make peace with God and let Him have what's left of my life."

Megan's hand crept to his brow again. It was cool and clammy.

"I don't think I'm going to die, if that's what you're thinking." He attempted a weak smile. "I want to be ready to live."

"I'll get Banjo." Forgetting her coat, Megan flew from the house to where Banjo and Wyatt were building a makeshift stable. "Steve wants you, Banjo," she panted. "Please come."

Banjo dropped the board he held and followed Megan. When they reached the house, she caught his sleeve.

"He says he wants to make his peace with God."

"What? Is he worse?"

"I don't think so. He says he wants to get ready to live, not to die, and he wants to live his life for the Lord."

"Thank God," he breathed. "If you'll get me your Bible, I'll go in."

Megan fetched the sacred book from her trunk and handed it

to Banjo. She listened as Banjo explained the story of salvation in the same simple way he had told her.

"Just tell God you're a sinner, and you want to claim the blood of Jesus to wash away your sin," he concluded.

Pain-wracked as he was, Steve's voice was strong.

"Lord, I want You to save me. I'm a rotten sinner. I know Jesus died for me, and I want You to take my life and make something useful from it. Amen."

Megan's eyes were misty when she looked up. She was surprised to see tears streaming down Banjo's face.

"I believe I could use some of that powder, Megan." Steve's face was ashen. His eyes closed as Megan scurried to bring him what he had asked for. He swallowed the medicine without opening his eyes, and sank back to the pillow.

Outside the bedroom door, Banjo drew a large red handkerchief from his pocket and loudly blew his nose.

"I tell you seein' someone born into the family of God is almost as good as bein' born again yourself," he said, wiping his eyes.

"God sent you here, Banjo," Megan said with conviction, love welling up inside of her. "I'm so glad He did." Her voice quavered.

"Thank Him, not me." His voice was husky. "All I did was tell you. God made it real in your hearts."

❧

The next evening Steve felt well enough to have Banjo visit for a few minutes.

"You wouldn't believe the shootin' that little lady did that morning," Banjo declared. "She saw Harrington draw and in one motion sighted and shot him in the arm. She hit what she shot at. Dead center."

"Is that right?" Steve looked over at Megan's faint blush.

"I did it before I thought." She was almost apologetic. "All I knew is that for some insane reason Beau had decided to kill you and I had to stop him."

Steve grinned at Banjo. "I'm glad she's on my side." He shifted to a more comfortable position. "What happened to Beau?"

"He lit a shuck. Took some stuff from the ranch and they

haven't seen hide nor hair of him since. Miss Susan's taking it pretty good, considerin'. I guess she's glad to have some peace after all the trouble. She's got spunk, that one. She made Curly foreman and had to talk with the men, Wyatt tells me. They're all staying on."

❧

The next long week, Megan nursed the man who was her husband in name only. It was gratifying to feel the closeness she sensed between them since he accepted Christ. They had quiet chats when he felt up to it, and she shared with him how God had given her a peace she could not explain through the past months of hardship.

She was with him every available minute of the day, feeding him hot soup when he could swallow it, boiling water for preparing fresh bandages, changing linen, and doling out pain powder until she fought collapse.

"Megan." Steve caught her hand as she passed by. "You're pushing yourself too hard. It'll be no help to me if you wear yourself out to the point where you have to be cared for yourself." He had shown encouraging signs of improvement the last two days. "Go up to the loft and lie down. Banjo can get me anything I need when he comes in from choring."

"But—"

He waved aside her protest.

"Go. That's an order."

It took her last bit of strength to climb the ladder and lie down on Steve's cot. Her head hurt. Her eyes closed before she touched the pillow. The house had a tomblike silence and it was fifteen hours before she opened her eyes again.

❧

"It looks good," Dr. Leatherwood said a few days later as he replaced the bandage. "We want it to heal from the inside out, not close over too soon or the wounds will fester." He winked at Steve. "You've got a good nurse there."

"I know it." Steve smiled at Megan. "She's done everything but pass her hand over the place and say, 'Be healed.' " Some of his original color had returned, though he still had spasms of pain now and then.

"How soon can I walk on it?"

"If you had a crutch you could get up now." The doctor buttoned his buffalo coat around his thick neck. "But under no circumstances are you to put any weight on it." He picked up his bag. "And take it slow at first. Fifteen minutes, then twenty, and so on."

"Will do." Steve shook Leatherwood's hand. "And thanks."

"Thanks to you, too," Steve said to Megan when the doctor had gone.

"You're getting better. That's thanks enough." Confused, Megan picked up his water pitcher and carried it to the spring to refill it. She yearned to be near him, but she wanted to run away from him at the same time. She was afraid. Afraid he might not care, afraid she was reading things into his words that didn't exist.

❧

"When Susan was here today she told me she and Wyatt are planning a December wedding," Megan remarked to Steve as she sat by his bed the next afternoon. She was cutting bandages from a large piece of white cloth.

"So soon?" He looked up from the newspaper Banjo had brought from town.

"It's long enough, after all they've been through. I know it hasn't been a year since her father died, but she's all alone with Beau leaving her like he did. Folks should understand." She avoided his eyes, so probing and somehow close these days. "I got a letter from Em, too."

"How's Jeremy?"

"Out of the woods, thank the Lord. I can't tell you how relieved I am. Em says he may be able to leave the sanitarium in the early spring." A clammy hand squeezed her heart at the thought of returning to Baltimore. "I'll be back sometime around then."

"Will you?" Something in his voice forced her to look at him. His gaze pierced to the core of her being.

She didn't know how to answer his question. She knew she must go back East no matter how much she longed to stay. She must look after Jeremy. Tormented thoughts cascaded over her as she stared at him, her throat too tight to make a sound. She looked away, cutting blindly at the cloth, wishing she could hide from him. He was torturing her by looking at her like that.

"Megan." He laid the paper aside and sat up. "Megan, don't run away from me. I can't stand it any longer. Please."

Against her will, she raised her head and met those eyes again.

"I don't want you to go, Megan. I want you to stay." He searched her troubled face for the answer. "I know I'm not the greatest fellow that ever came along, but I love you, Megan. With all my heart and soul, I love you. All this," a wide sweep of his hand included all that lay around them, "would be worthless to me if you weren't here."

Her lip began to quiver, and her eyes filled with tears. She pressed her eyes tight and looked down as the tears spilled down her cheeks.

"My dear." Anxiety clouded his features. "I'm sorry if I've upset you."

"No. It's not that." She shook her head, fumbling for her handkerchief. "I just. . .don't know what to. . .it's what I've been asking the Lord for ever since I've been saved. Of course I'll stay."

Sunbeams broke through the clouds like the first bright rays after a storm. He reached out and grasped her wrist, pulling her to him. Her scissors clattered to the floor, but no one heard.

"I can't believe it's true," Megan whispered in a moment. A lone tear trickled down her cheek, inconsistent with her glorious smile.

Steve took her handkerchief and dabbed at the spot.

"If you're happy, why do you keep crying?"

"I don't know," she said with a little laugh. "I can't help it."

"We'll send for Jeremy as soon as he's released."

"And Em," Megan added. "Don't forget Em." She nestled her head on his strong shoulder.

"Certainly Em. When you answered my ad, you were so scared and brave at the same time that it changed something inside me. I wanted to help you, to protect you from all the trouble you were having. That's why I was so anxious for you to come with me."

"Why didn't you tell me before this? There were times when I thought I'd die if you didn't care."

"When I got to know you I saw what a conscientious, uncorrupted person you are, Megan. I'm nothing but a riverboat gambler. I couldn't ask you to stay with the likes of me."

Megan shook her head. "I never felt that way."

"Back then that possibility never occurred to me, but when I turned my life over to God all those guilty feelings disappeared. I began to wonder if I may have a chance with you now that we share the same faith." He gave her a loving squeeze. "I want to build a new life, Megan. With you."

He tilted her chin up so he could look into her eyes. "There's only one thing I regret."

"There is?" Flickering doubt crossed her face.

"Yes. I can't ask you to marry me."

"Oh." The smile reappeared. "Well, you could say it anyway."

"Will you be my wife, Megan?" Infinite tenderness was in the question.

"Yes."

The fear, the empty longing, the anguish were rooted out and washed away by a flood tide of joy.

৯

Whistling softly to himself, Banjo came into the house intending to ask Steve how he wanted the stable door set. When he reached the open door of Megan's room, he drew back. It took only a fraction of a second for him to realize how matters stood. Without hesitating he tiptoed out of the house and quietly closed the door behind him.

When he reached the middle of the yard he couldn't hold the joy in any longer. He let out a thundering, "Eee-hah!" and raised his hat in salute. A song gushed out with all his strength behind it.

> "I will praise Him!
> I will praise Him!
> Praise the Lamb for sinners slain;

Give Him glory all ye people,
For His blood can wash away each stain!"*

Megan heard his words, and her spirit joined in the benediction. She wanted to shout.

---

* *Great Hymns of the Faith*, ed. John W. Peterson (Grand Rapids: Singspiration Music, 1980), p. 464.

A Letter To Our Readers

Dear Reader:

In order that we might better contribute to your reading enjoyment, we would appreciate your taking a few minutes to respond to the following questions. When completed, please return to the following:

Rebecca Germany, Managing Editor
Heartsong Presents
P.O. Box 719
Uhrichsville, Ohio 44683

1. Did you enjoy reading *Megan's Choice*?
   ❏ Very much. I would like to see more books
      by this author!
   ❏ Moderately
      I would have enjoyed it more if _____

   _____

2. Are you a member of **Heartsong Presents**? ❏Yes ❏No
   If no, where did you purchase this book? _____

   _____

3. What influenced your decision to purchase this
   book? (Check those that apply.)

   ❏ Cover   ❏ Back cover copy

   ❏ Title   ❏ Friends

   ❏ Publicity   ❏ Other_____

4. How would you rate, on a scale from 1 (poor) to 5
   (superior), the cover design? _____

5. On a scale from 1 (poor) to 10 (superior), please rate the following elements.

___Heroine ___Plot

___ Hero ___ Inspirational theme

___ Setting ___Secondary characters

6. What settings would you like to see covered in **Heartsong Presents** books?_____

_____

_____

7. What are some inspirational themes you would like to see treated in future books?_____

_____

_____

8. Would you be interested in reading other **Heartsong Presents** titles? ❑ Yes ❑ No

9. Please check your age range:
   ❑ Under 18 ❑ 18-24 ❑ 25-34
   ❑ 35-45 ❑ 46-55 ❑ Over 55

10. How many hours per week do you read? _____

Name _____

Occupation _____

Address _____

City _____ State _____ Zip _____

·······Hearts♥ng ·······

Heart♥ng Presents
Love Stories Are Rated G!

That's for godly, gratifying, and of course, great! If you love a thrilling love story, but don't appreciate the sordidness of some popular paperback romances, **Heartsong Presents** is for you. In fact, **Heartsong Presents** is the *only inspirational romance book club*, the only one featuring love stories where Christian faith is the primary ingredient in a marriage relationship.

Sign up today to receive your first set of four, never before published Christian romances. Send no money now; you will receive a bill with the first shipment. You may cancel at any time without obligation, and if you aren't completely satisfied with any selection, you may return the books for an immediate refund!

Imagine. . .four new romances every four weeks—two historical, two contemporary—with men and women like you who long to meet the one God has chosen as the love of their lives. . .all for the low price of $9.97 postpaid.

To join, simply complete the coupon below and mail to the address provided. **Heartsong Presents** romances are rated G for another reason: They'll arrive *Godspeed!*